Let everybody know what you thought of this book!

It was great!	It was okay.	It was awful.

D1525812

Setting the Stage for Love

RONI DENHOLTZ

Brooke thinks William is a friend, but he wants something more. Can a rescued cat help bring them together?

There was a stepladder nearby and when she indicated it, William obligingly dragged it over. She went up a few steps and easily rehung the curtain where it sagged.

She was conscious that he was behind her, holding the ladder steadily. She put one foot down on the next step, then the other. His arms surrounded her.

Her heart rate sped up.

Brooke turned. She was much shorter than William, but on the ladder, she stood slightly above him. She inched down another step. Their eyes met at the same level.

His gaze locked on hers.

Brooke felt zapped by an electric current.

"Brooke!" Connie's voice interrupted the private moment.

William let go, and Brooke stepped down, until she reached the floor. Her head spun. The way William had looked at her, as if he wanted to kiss her…

She felt a little dazed. Because, for a moment, she had *wanted* him to kiss her.

DEDICATION

For My Nieces and Nephews, in birth order:

Eric Samuel Denholtz
David Joseph Silber
Tracy Lyn Denholtz
Lauren Gabrielle Silber
Melissa Beth Denholtz
Conner Ian Klein
Arielle Trina Klein
Natalie Hannah Paitchel

With love from Aunt Roni

ACKNOWLEDGMENTS

A big thank you to my editor, Gina Ardito
and my cover guru and formatter, Judi Fennell!

CHAPTER I

"Brooke!"

Brooke Perez stared at the man who had called out her name, barely able to keep her mouth from falling open in surprise.

She stood in the entryway of the home of her brother's maybe-girlfriend, Nicole Vitarelli. Coming toward her with a familiar spring in his step was William Jenkins—her first serious boyfriend. An expression of astonishment spread over his face as he approached.

"William?" she squeaked as her heartbeat accelerated. It was wonderful to see him! Using the control her actress mother had taught her long ago, she automatically modulated her voice and repeated, "William?" in a softer, more even tone. She followed his name with a wide smile.

"Hi, Brooke!" His voice sounded full of enthusiasm. "Jeremy, it's great to see you again."

She barely registered her brother, Jeremy, passing the salad they'd brought to a pretty, dark-haired young woman, who stood in the foyer. William reached out and gave Brooke a huge hug.

When she pulled back, she couldn't stop staring at him. William Jenkins! He looked hot!

His dark blond hair was shorter than it was in high school and college. His bluish-gray eyes and wide smile remained as dazzling as when he was younger. He seemed taller than she recalled, though. And despite the large New York Jets football sweatshirt he wore, it was evident his shoulders were even broader than they'd been when he was a youth. While he looked very much the same, there was a certain air of maturity surrounding him now. He was no longer a young, attractive guy, but a man fully grown, at ease with himself and the world. And really good-looking.

Something clicked on inside Brooke, like a stage spotlight highlighting a place that had lain dark for a long time.

"…my sister Brooke…" Jeremy's words pierced her reverie. Stop gawking like a teenager, she ordered herself. But she couldn't help the smile glued on her face.

"I guess you two know each other?" The dark-haired woman smiling at Jeremy transferred her gaze to Brooke and William. "What a coincidence."

"Yes. William and I knew each other in high school," Brooke said. "He was my first major boyfriend."

"How funny!" the woman remarked.

Brooke forced herself to transfer her attention to the petite, pretty woman Jeremy was attracted to. He'd told her Nicole had a cooking series on the local cable TV station, and Jeremy helped out by appearing on her show, "A Taste of Romance," which featured romantic dinners. Nicole and her sister lived across the street from Jeremy. Nicole's sister was the other dark-haired woman in the room.

"This is Nicole," Jeremy introduced. Brooke shook Nicole's hand. "And Nicole's sister, Marla..." Jeremy continued, waving at the woman who looked a lot like Nicole, but was slightly taller, "and Marla's friend, Scott." A dark-haired guy sat near Marla. They stood and crowded around, shaking hands and exchanging greetings.

"I'm so glad to meet you," Brooke said. She'd sort of badgered Jeremy to introduce her to Nicole. It had been a long time since she'd heard her younger brother sound so enthusiastic about a woman, and Brooke was eager to meet Nicole. Jeremy had told her the sisters were making dinner for several people, and it would be a great opportunity for her to get to meet Nicole at last. Somehow, he'd finagled an invitation for both of them. Now, here they were, with the simple salad they'd brought along. Even Brooke and Jeremy were capable of making that culinary contribution to dinner!

"Have a seat," Nicole said to Brooke with a smile. "I'll just put this salad in the fridge."

Jeremy followed Nicole, and William drew Brooke to the couch. "Wow, I can't believe it. Nicole told me some more people were coming for dinner, but I didn't know it was you and Jeremy. What a great surprise!" They sat cozily close. "How are you, Brooke?"

"Fine. How do you know Nicole?" she asked.

"I'm a videographer for the Morris County cable station," William replied. "I'm assigned to Nicole's cooking show, and every once in a while, I get a great home-cooked meal. I almost didn't believe it when Jeremy appeared on the show. We barely had time to

3

talk, so I was hoping next time to catch up with him and hear more about what you're doing. This is even better--I get to see you in person!"

Brooke took a deep breath. She felt as if she had stepped onto the stage and was now bathed in a rainbow of light. Which made no sense at all.

William had been her boyfriend—her first long term one—back in high school. She'd broken up with him amidst teenage confusion and upheaval. But after some time, they'd ended up casual friends. In college, they dated others and saw each other occasionally, but since then, they hadn't really stayed in touch. The last time she'd seen him must have been six years ago, a brief and accidental encounter. He'd been with a woman she didn't know, in a store in their hometown.

She didn't want to think about all that now. She deliberately chose to concentrate on the present. And with that thought, an idea burst into her brain. William…an old friend. This was *exactly* what she needed at this point in her life. After that fiasco with Nate, she'd sworn off men. But maybe an old friend…

"The last time I saw you, you were a redhead," William said, interrupting her train of thought. He cocked his head slightly. "I like your natural color better."

Brooke grinned. She enjoyed changing her hair color to suit her mood, but for the last year had left it her naturally blond color, with an occasional highlight of blue or purple in the front. She wore it shorter than she used to and wondered what he thought of the style.

"You look great," she said, deciding she'd feel more comfortable if the emphasis was on him and not her. "How's your family?"

"My sister teaches deaf children up in Sussex County," William said. "My parents…" He shrugged. "They're okay."

Familiar sympathy tugged at Brooke. His mother and father had both worked for large corporations for years. They often traveled, separately, leaving William and his older sister with various housekeepers. Both the kids had resented their parents' total devotion to their jobs, feeling they came in second place in their parents' lives, which was true, Brooke often observed. Although the Jenkinses were well off and their children had everything they needed, they weren't there for them in the way her own parents were: at music concerts and play performances, at science exhibits and soccer games. Her parents ate dinner at home a large percentage of the time, despite their busy schedules.

"My dad had some health issues and retired last year," William continued. "He's golfing a lot now, and I actually get to see him occasionally. I think he feels badly that he didn't spend much time with us when we were younger," he confided, his voice dropping. "My mom is still working, although she doesn't travel as much as she used to." He shrugged again, but Brooke guessed from his tone he didn't resent them as much as he did when he was younger.

"Dinner's almost ready," Nicole said, interrupting the moment.

Perhaps they'd have more time to talk about his family later.

She hoped he wouldn't bring up hers. Brooke knew Jeremy hadn't told Nicole about their famous family, preferring Nicole get to know him for himself.

Before she could let William know not to say anything, he grasped her hand.

Her skin tingled where they touched and the tingling spread like wildfire from her hand, up her arm, and through her entire body, warming her from the roots of her hair to her toes.

"Thanks for asking." His voice was husky, his expression warm. "Everyone here calls me Will, by the way."

Will. She'd have to get used to that.

Brooke swallowed. "I want to hear about your job, and how you're doing," she said quickly as he pulled her to her feet. A change of subject might avoid the topic of the famous Perez family.

William was tall, and next to him, she felt small and unexpectedly feminine. As they followed Scott into the dining room, he talked about his job, doing video for the nearby county cable station. A lot of feature programs, he said, some hard news, and he enjoyed it. He'd worked in Boston, in Connecticut, and Maryland, but was happy to get the job in New Jersey and come back "home."

"I'm renting a small house in Roxbury with a friend of mine and planning to buy one soon. But enough about me, I want to hear about you."

Brooke felt torn. She wanted to hear more about him. On the other hand, her brother had engineered this gathering so she could meet Nicole. She hadn't heard Jeremy so enthusiastic about any woman for ages, especially after one had broken his heart; and she wanted to learn more about his potential girlfriend.

If she sat between William and Nicole, she might be able to pay attention to both.

"How about we eat, and I'll fill you in later?" she asked.

"Okay. Eating is good," he replied.

For a moment, she flashed back to the teenager he'd been, with his young, eager face and friendly smile.

A strong yearning called to her, the kind she'd felt for him a long, long time ago. It was over thirteen years since they'd both been seventeen, but that smile brought it all back: the dates, the nervousness before a big dance, the awkward but sweet kisses.

Marla handed William a bowl heaped with a rice and vegetable mixture, and as Brooke watched him, he brought it into the dining room before she turned to help carry in some salad dressings.

Hmmm...maybe that smile had been for the food and his hostesses, not for her.

She'd never been that interested in learning to cook more than a basic meal, but suddenly wished she knew how to cook something special.

***

Will regarded Brooke as she passed her brother the salad. The moment she'd entered Nicole's home, he'd been riveted, unable to keep his eyes off her.

It wasn't that Brooke Perez was beautiful. She was, but the other two women there, Nicole and Marla, were as well. And it wasn't that Brooke looked artsy and intriguing. There was something about Brooke— some quality that made a man sit up and take notice.

She was petite and looked a lot like her mother, with blond hair with a small wave at the end, and bright green eyes. Her generous mouth smiled often, and her eyes sparkled. But it wasn't just her face.

Brooke had a certain flair that always made her stand out, even among dozens of attractive women. Today, she wore a yellow, purple, and black sweater and black jeans that hugged her slim figure. She didn't need the dramatic and colorful clothes to draw attention to herself, although she had always dressed in an artistic fashion. Her makeup was more subtle than he remembered—not that she needed any, he thought. Brooke Perez looked gorgeous, no matter what.

She met his eyes, and smiled.

He smiled back.

"Wow," Marla said. "This is a funny coincidence, you and Jeremy knowing Will."

Guilt rumbled through Will.

It wasn't a coincidence.

What would Brooke say if she found out he'd deliberately arranged the whole event? Their dinner, on a cool Sunday in September, was not a mere coincidence.

Will bent his head, concentrating on the delicious food, and hoped Brooke didn't guess his thoughts. She complimented Nicole and Marla on the brisket they'd cooked. He tasted the meat in its spicy sauce. Heavenly.

A couple of times, Nicole had taken pity on him when he complained about bachelorhood and the fact he wasn't a very good cook, and she'd had him over for dinner. She was a superior cook, and he'd never failed to be impressed. He liked Nicole, but he'd always regarded her as a friend, and he knew she felt the same way.

On Friday, while videotaping Nicole's cooking show at the station, he'd been surprised but pleased when Jeremy Perez showed up. It turned out Jeremy was playing the part of Nicole's boyfriend on the show.

It hadn't taken long for William to realize Jeremy and Nicole were attracted to each other, despite their fake relationship. When he spoke to Jeremy alone after the taping, Jeremy had confided Nicole didn't know about the famous Perez family, and he wanted to keep it that way. Jeremy wanted people to know and like him, without being impressed by his soap-opera-star mother and famous doctor dad.

Will had agreed not to say a word to Nicole, but had one request in return. He'd asked Jeremy to get him together with Brooke.

Oddly enough, he'd dreamed about Brooke a month or so ago. Inspired, he found her on Facebook, but he'd been afraid to send her a message. What if she wasn't interested in seeing him? He'd decided it would be better if he could somehow connect with her another way.

And then he'd run into Jeremy, and the perfect opportunity had presented itself!

For the first time, he wondered how Brooke would feel about this set-up. She'd always prized honesty in her friends, and he didn't want to let her know how he and Jeremy had arranged this meeting, practically inviting themselves to dinner. They were lucky Nicole and Marla were so warm and welcoming.

"So what do you think about the Giants' chances against San Francisco?" Jeremy asked. Will snapped back to the present.

"William is an avid Jets fan," Brooke reminded her brother.

"We always call him Will at the station," Nicole said lightly. She turned to him. "Which do you prefer?"

He shrugged. "Will, William—whatever. I think the Giants are going to beat the Forty-Niners," he answered Jeremy. He grinned at Brooke. "And you're right." He indicated his sweatshirt. "The Jets are still my favorite team. I'll be watching their next game closely."

The conversation revolved around various football teams. The meal was delicious, but even with the interesting conversation and outstanding food, Will found himself focusing on Brooke.

After their break-up in high school, they hadn't seen each other for a while, then had become casually friendly again near the end of college. Would she still think of him as a casual friend after this evening? He'd known from the minute he saw her again he'd like to take her out. He felt more than a casual interest in Brooke. He guessed there was only one way to find out if she had similar leanings. He'd get her phone number and ask her out.

With dinner over, the six of them proceeded to clean up before dessert, still debating which teams were likely to do well that season. At one point, Brooke handed him an empty platter, and their fingers brushed.

A vibration spread through his hand from that simple touch.

He didn't get a chance to speak with her one-on-one, though, until people were getting ready to leave.

"I'd really like to hear about you, and your work, and how you're doing," he said as he moved closer to Brooke. "How about we get together soon?" Yeah, that sounded like an invitation from a sophisticated man. But then, maybe she'd be more likely to go out with him if she regarded it as a friends-getting-together thing instead of a dating thing.

"I'd like that."

Hey, that was something! He couldn't help smiling. "What's your phone number?" he asked, pulling his iPhone from his pocket.

As he programmed Brooke's cell number into his phone, the conversation turned to TV shows, and someone mentioned soap operas. Beside him, Will felt Jeremy tense.

"Oh, I like to watch *As the Universe Spins* and *All My Relatives*," Brooke said casually. Too casually. He knew Brooke, and he knew she was acting. She was a good actress, really, and had starred in several high school productions. He suspected she was cooperating with Jeremy's wish to keep quiet about their famous family.

Brooke had something to do with theatre set designs now, and he was eager to ask her about her job. But that would have to wait for their next conversation, when they were alone.

Marla agreed about the soaps, and Nicole didn't seem overly interested in the topic. He sensed Jeremy relax.

He walked out with Brooke and her brother, and she said, "It was great to run into you."

"I feel the same." A brisk wind stirred her hair, and he had a desire to touch the blond strands. "I'll call you on Tuesday."

11

She unexpectedly stepped forward and gave him a friendly hug. "Okay."

In those few seconds, Brooke felt so good in his arms he could have stayed that way for quite a while. He had to force himself not to draw her closer, but to keep the hug friendly and short.

Behind her, Jeremy winked.

She stepped back.

"I'll talk to you soon!" Will declared, then headed to his car. He was already thinking about what he'd say when he called on Tuesday while he unlocked the door and climbed inside his Jeep.

He'd have to keep his knowledge about Jeremy's family from Nicole, he thought as he started the car.

And keep quiet about arranging this meeting.

CHAPTER II

On Tuesday afternoon, Brooke's ringing cell phone, playing Madonna's "Vogue," startled her.

She sat in the rather cramped office she shared with two other adjunct professors at Quemby Mountain College, a small college in northwestern New Jersey. She'd been looking over her lesson plans for her Thursday classes, History of the Theatre I and Introduction to Stage Scenery and Design.

She almost knocked over her mug of mint tea as she grabbed her iPhone. That particular ringtone was used for general callers. She'd assigned other ringtones for her sister, brothers and close friends, so this was someone else. Caller ID showed an unfamiliar number.

"Hello?" she asked cautiously. Her students had her email and voicemail through the college, but not her personal cell number.

"Brooke! How are you?"

William's voice instantly brightened the gray, rainy afternoon.

"Hi!" Brooke replied, relaxing back into her chair. "I'm fine. How are you?"

From the bookcase near his desk where he stood,

Bert Whelan, Director of Theatre Productions at Quemby, shot her a glance, his eyebrows raised.

She sighed inwardly. As an experienced actor and director, Bert was in tune to every inflection and nuance of a person's voice and posture. He only taught one class at Quemby besides his directing, so he wasn't in the office much, but he'd been working on something all afternoon and now was obviously eavesdropping.

Brooke gave him a look, and he grinned.

"I'm good," William replied. "I was wondering if you were free and we could get together this weekend."

She'd been speculating if he'd ask to see her on a weeknight or a weekend. She'd hoped for Friday, since she had tentative plans for Saturday.

"How about Friday?" she suggested.

"I'm taping a show—not Nicole's, another cooking show. Maybe afterwards, if it's not too late?"

A thought occurred to her. "Do you remember my friend, Connie Wu? From NYU?" She'd been best friends with Connie all through college, and they'd remained close ever since. "She's doing the lighting for a new off-off-Broadway production, and I'm going to see it Saturday night. I'm pretty sure I can get an extra ticket, if you want to go."

Bert raised his eyebrows, then waggled them.

Brooke made a face and rotated her seat so Bert couldn't observe her expressions.

"That would be great!" William declared. "Why don't we go into the city in the afternoon, wander around, and have an early dinner before the show?"

"Perfect." She enjoyed going into the city, and

spending time with William was always fun. "There are a couple of gallery exhibits I wouldn't mind seeing, if you feel like it."

They set a time for William to pick her up, deciding to take a train in, and Brooke gave him the address of her condo in Hackettstown.

"It's easy to find," she began.

"I have a GPS. I'll find it," he told her. "I'm looking forward to seeing you, Brooke."

Something inside her softened at his words. "Me, too," she said, reminding herself he was a good friend, and they always had a nice time together.

And spending time with a friend was exactly what she needed at this point.

She heard someone call "Will" on his end.

"I gotta get going," he said. "Break's over, and we need to retape something."

"I'll see you Saturday," she said. "If there's any problem getting tickets, I'll let you know."

"See you then," he said. "Bye."

She ended the call.

"New boyfriend?" Bert asked.

"Nosy!" Brooke accused, laughing. Bert was interested in everyone's business. He was in his mid-sixties and a nice guy. He'd had plenty of years of experience directing plays all over, including on Broadway. He was now semi-retired, teaching the one class at Quemby, and directing the major shows here. They worked together, since she did scenery and stage design, although she also worked with the smaller theatre groups on campus that were for theatre and non-theatre majors; and she taught three classes. "No, he's just an old friend from my hometown I ran into

15

last weekend, and we're going to get together to see Connie's new production."

"I asked a few friends about it when you mentioned your friend was doing the lighting. They said last week's opening went well," Bert said, finally selecting a book and returning to his desk. He kept up with the New York theatre scene. "I might try to see it in a couple of weeks."

"Yes, Connie was pleased." Brooke had noticed the time on her iPhone was already 4:15. "I better finish my work. I'm meeting my brother for dinner."

"That's right, it's Tuesday," Bert observed.

Brooke tried to meet Jeremy every Tuesday for dinner, unless one of them had to work late or had another commitment. He lived only a few minutes from her, and he was only a year and a half younger than Brooke.

She wondered what Jeremy would think of her going out with William. Not that they were going out, she reminded herself.

Still, that didn't explain the magnified anticipation she already felt about the weekend.

***

Brooke pulled her car into her condo's garage on Wednesday afternoon, noting the big moving truck next door. Her neighbor, Fredericka, must be moving.

She got out of her car and went down the driveway to say goodbye. She hardly knew Fredericka. The older woman had lived here since before Brooke moved in two years ago, and she didn't see her outside much. As she approached, two moving men placed a luxurious-looking leather sectional couch in the truck. Another two men carried a large screen TV down the sidewalk. It looked almost new.

"You're moving?" Brooke asked Fredericka, who stood nearby, frowning.

"I have to." She grimaced. "The bank foreclosed on my condo, and I have to move out by the end of the week."

Surprised, Brooke stared at her neighbor.

"I lost my job right after I bought this." Fredericka waved at her condo. "And I haven't made a payment since. Well, it was fun while it lasted."

Brooke tried not to show her astonishment at Fredericka's cavalier attitude. She forced herself not to look at the expensive TV or furniture. It seemed Fredericka had spent her money on furniture instead of her mortgage.

"Where are you moving to?" Brooke asked, wondering if she was moving in with relatives. She knew the woman was divorced and had two grown sons, but she barely saw them around. They either lived far or didn't see her often.

She caught a whiff of Fredericka's perfume, one her Aunt Lorraine always wore, and she recognized it as very expensive. Apparently, Fredericka spent money on designer scents, too.

"Texas. I have some family there," Fredericka said. "Oh, can you do me a favor, hon?"

Brooke hesitated, juggling her tote, which held the papers she wanted to grade that night. She hardly knew Fredericka and was afraid of what the older woman would ask.

"The nearest animal shelter is full," Fredericka

17

Roni Denholtz

continued. "Can you find a home for my cat? I don't want to just leave him outside."

"Leave him outside?" Brooke's stomach lurched. Her family had had both dogs and cats while she was growing up, and she loved animals. She was appalled by the idea Fredericka could abandon her cat. "You can't leave him outside to fend for himself!" Many times she'd come home and seen the gray cat lounging by the window, peering out curiously at the world. "He's a housecat, he'd never survive. He's not used to the weather getting colder or scrounging for food—"

Fredericka waved a hand. "I know, I know. But I don't know what else to do."

"Can't you take him with you?" Brooke said, her heart sinking.

"Nah. It's a long trip, and I don't even know for sure where I'll be living. He's a nice cat, only a couple of years old. I'm sure you can find him a home quickly," she cajoled.

Then why couldn't you? Brooke thought. Aloud, she said, "Have you tried your vet?"

The woman shook her head. "I owe her money. I doubt she'd help me."

But you managed to buy a brand new TV. "Maybe you could sell some furniture." She forced herself to sound calm, rather than furious.

Fredericka shook her head. "I already sold one bedroom set. I'm not parting with anything else."

Well, it looked like the TV was a priority. Wind gusted suddenly, cooling her hot cheeks. She gritted her teeth and glanced at Fredericka's front window. The cat peered out, and she could swear he looked anxious, as if he knew his fate was up in the air.

18

Perhaps he did. A lot of people believed animals had ESP, and Brooke was one of them. She couldn't stand to think of the poor thing fending for himself.

"All right," she said with a sigh. "Do you have food and a litter box?"

"Of course, doll, of course. I even have his medical records. He won't be any trouble, and I'm sure it will be no time until you find him a home." Fredericka beamed.

"Just give me a chance to get these things inside, and I'll be right over," Brooke told her.

A few minutes later, she was handed the cat. Fredericka said he was named Tiger. He was medium-sized, soft, and had lovely pale green eyes. The minute she took hold of him, Tiger let out a deep purr.

Fredericka patted him. "You be good now." Then she gave Brooke a bag of food and a large shopping bag with a litter box, kitty litter, and a couple of toys in it. "He won't be any trouble. Thanks, doll."

What was she getting into? Brooke wondered. But she couldn't stand by while a helpless animal was abandoned.

***

An hour later, the moving truck make a loud huffing noise, and she looked up from her desk to see it slowly pull away.

She'd called three local animal shelters. All were full and had no room for any cats, so she'd put Tiger on waiting lists at each one. The people at each had been kind but sad when they explained it was difficult to find homes for adult cats, and they had no room in the shelters at the moment for Tiger. Health codes meant they were strict about not overcrowding the shelters.

The four vets she had called each had cats and kittens they were trying to adopt out and no place for him, either.

She sighed. She would have to use word of mouth to find him a home.

She almost jumped when she felt something soft against her foot, until she realized it was Tiger. Glancing down, she met his look. He made a funny noise.

"Are you hungry? Okay, I'll feed you."

It was almost five, and she wouldn't be able to call anyone else today. At least she knew from experience how to take care of a cat. She'd closed the doors to her basement with its family room full of art projects, crafts and scenery stuff—all things he'd probably love to get tangled in—and had closed off her bedroom and the guestroom upstairs. That still left her combined living room/dining room and kitchen, plus the home office, for Tiger to wander in and out— plenty of room for one cat. So far, he'd spent most of the last hour exploring her home office as she talked on the phone, playing with a stuffed toy mouse among his possessions, and sitting on her large chair near the window, staring outside.

She stopped to scratch him behind his ears. "Poor thing," she whispered.

He looked at her, then purred.

She went into the kitchen, and he followed her. "I'm going to Jazzercise in a little while," she told him firmly. "You'll have to hang out here by yourself."

He meowed.

She recalled William and his sister had always wanted a cat or a dog, although their parents hadn't let them have any pets. Maybe William would want a cat now?

***

Brooke wrote a neat A-minus on the paper, jotted down a few encouraging comments, and then put her pen down and stretched. She still liked to correct papers the old-fashioned way, rather than on a computer, and had her students print them out and hand them in to her that way.

A glance at her computer screen showed her it was nearly nine-thirty. She'd accomplished a lot in the last four and a half hours. After Jazzercise and a shower, she'd had a quick late dinner, then settled down to grade the short papers her students had turned in today. She could work some more, but she had reached a good breaking point and would have time to grade more papers tomorrow.

She glanced out the window. Lights around the condo complex glowed in the dark. A car pulled into a driveway across from her building, and a neighbor passed by the nearest streetlight, walking her terrier. A nice, normal, quiet evening.

Except a cat had joined her. He lay curled up in the chair by the window, fast asleep. As she gazed at him, Tiger raised his head, blinked, then settled back down and went promptly back to sleep.

Well, he certainly didn't seem too upset by his change in homes. Which did surprise her, since one of

21

the cats her family had owned had been so scared he'd hidden in the bathroom for two days when they'd moved to their larger house—the one her parents still lived in.

At least Tiger wasn't living outside, alone and frightened and fending for himself. She got angry all over again, thinking Fredericka might have abandoned him. She wondered if the woman would really have done that, or if she was just saying so, hoping Brooke could be manipulated into taking him. She guessed she'd never know. But she was glad she'd been able to help the cat, even if it was temporary.

The cat had trusted Fredericka to care for him, and he'd been let down. How could someone give away an animal who was part of their household?

She picked up her bottle of water and tilted it to her lips, taking a cool drink. Perhaps, she and Tiger were kindred spirits. Hadn't she been let down by Nathan Halstead?

Nate. The thought of him sent a burning sensation of embarrassment, anger, and yes, hurt, sweeping through her.

She'd met Nate in May, at the end of the last spring semester, at a party one of the deans was hosting. He was the new coach of the men's tennis team, hired just that year. Since she didn't have much to do with the athletic department at the other end of campus, she had never met him before, although she'd heard of him. He'd been a tennis pro for a while until an injury had caused him to switch careers to coaching and teaching.

He'd flirted with her openly at the party, but she'd found him amusing and didn't mind. He'd asked her out. Pretty soon, they were going out several times a week, and she had begun to wonder if her summer romance was turning serious. She really enjoyed his company, and Nate seemed so considerate. He'd even, out of the blue, bought her expensive gold and ruby earrings.

She wondered about the fact he usually took her to expensive, but out of the way, places. College teachers, especially new ones, and tennis coaches didn't draw big salaries. She'd speculated that perhaps, like her, he came from a family with money and had made some wise investments.

But in the first week in August, he'd come to see the local production she was helping with in a nearby community. During the intermission, Dorothy, one of the women playing a secondary role, caught sight of Brooke talking to him. When Brooke returned backstage, she had asked Brooke if Nate had come to see her.

Brooke had answered yes, and Dorothy had frowned. There was no chance to ask her about it until the show was over.

When she did approach Dorothy, the woman had hesitated, then spewed the information. "Did you know Nathan Halstead is married?"

"He is?" Brooke had been aghast. *Married*? Nate? And he'd never told her, never hinted…

"Yes. To that pop singer, what's her name…? Shanna something. She's off in Europe, touring for most of the summer."

So Nate had used her, amusing himself while his wife ran around Europe.

Brooke had been livid. She'd marched outside

and confronted Nate, who readily admitted he was married. "But I thought you knew. I thought, like me, you just wanted to have a good time."

She didn't! Brooke had given him a piece of her mind and told him never to call her again.

But she'd been hurt as well as angry. And mad at herself. How could she have been so stupid? She wasn't a naïve young kid. She was a woman who had dated, was comfortable around men. Some people called her sophisticated.

She should have known--should have recognized the signs!

She was never dating again. Or, at least, not for a long time.

As she sat, William's face flashed into her mind. With William, she felt secure. He was an old friend, nice and dependable. She could go out with him, have fun, and not worry about anything. She could take him to a show or a party if she wanted an escort. And unlike Nate, he was honest.

Just what she needed right now.

***

"He is a nice cat," Adrielle Morgan said, leaning down to pet Tiger.

Brooke shut the front door behind Adrielle and led the way into her living room. "Yes, he is. So far, no one's called, although I put up some flyers about him."

"I wish I could take him." Adrielle sighed. "But no pets allowed in the apartment Tina and I are renting."

Adrielle, who was a senior at Quemby, was the set designer for the next student-run production and a theatre major, specializing in scene and set design. She'd wanted to see the old lamp from the forties Brooke had found in an antique shop, so she could try to find similar type pieces for the mystery play they'd be doing soon.

"Your brother fixed it?" she asked, peering through her trendy eyeglasses at the Art-Deco black lamp.

"Yes. The cord was frayed, and I didn't want to start a fire," Brooke said.

Adrielle took out her phone and snapped a picture of the lamp. "Okay, I'll take this photo with me when I go to the thrift shops tomorrow. Want to come?"

"I can't." Brooke loved hunting for just the right object to help set a scene, like this lamp, and she enjoyed Adrielle's company. She considered the younger woman a friend. But it was Friday afternoon. She had no classes on Friday and usually saved the day for her favorite scenery work. Tomorrow was Saturday and her trip into New York with William. "I'm going into the city."

"What are you doing?" Adrielle asked eagerly.

"Going to browse around some galleries with an old friend, then on to see my friend's work in that off-off Broadway show she's doing." She frowned suddenly, then confessed, "I don't know what to wear. The weather's supposed to be cool."

"Want help picking something out?" Adrielle asked.

"Yes, I could use some advice. I can't decide between two outfits. C'mon, I'll show you."

They went upstairs to Brooke's bedroom, which she'd painted a soothing light aquamarine that reminded her of the ocean. She wasn't surprised when Tiger followed them.

The cat seemed to like following her around when she was home. It made Brooke wonder if he'd been lonely for much of his life. He usually found a place to sit where he could watch her. She'd bought him a couple of small carpeted cat perches yesterday that he seemed to like, and often when she was reading, or watching TV, or on the computer, he would snooze on one. Other times, she'd find him gazing out the window, and she wondered if he missed Fredericka.

"I've always had cats," Adrielle said as Brooke indicated the outfits tossed on her bed. "Tiger looks like he's happy here."

That made Brooke pause. "You think?" She turned to stare at Tiger.

He stared back, his tail twitching ever so slightly.

Adrielle nodded. "Maybe you should keep him."

Brooke turned to regard her, then the cat. "I don't know," she said slowly. She'd been trying to find him a home—he really was a nice, mellow cat—and she hadn't really thought about having a pet, except in fleeting moments. She was busy, running around with classes and work and volunteer theatre productions. "I'm not home a lot."

"Cats can be alone more than dogs," Adrielle pointed out. "And you can always get another one to keep him company. Okay, show me your outfits. I'm meeting Matt for dinner in a little while."

Brooke showed her the two outfits she'd placed

on the bed. The first was an emerald green sweater she'd bought recently with a cream-colored T shirt to wear underneath. The green color, she thought, brought out the green in her eyes. She'd paired it with her favorite old black boots, which were very comfortable for walking, and sleek black pants.

The second was a white sweater; a long, favorite scarf she'd bought in London a few years ago in shades of white, gold, brown and rust; and brown pants with simple low brown shoes that she also knew would be comfortable.

"I like the green best," Adrielle said.

Tiger jumped up on the chair in her room and meowed, as if in agreement, then began washing a paw.

Brooke studied the outfits. "I think you're right." She leaned over to finger the smooth texture of the emerald green sweater.

Adrielle quirked her brows. "I'm curious. You said this was an old friend you're going to the city with. Why the big decision about what to wear?"

Good question, Brooke thought. "I just want to look nice. You never know who you'll meet at the theatre."

Adrielle accepted the explanation.

But after she left, Brooke wondered herself. What was the big deal? Was she dressing to impress William?

CHAPTER III

The doorbell's chime interrupted Brooke in the middle of pulling on her sweater.

She'd decided last night to wear a completely different outfit, one she hadn't shown to Adrielle. Then this morning, she'd changed her mind and gone back to the black and emerald ensemble.

She glanced at the clock, exactly twelve-thirty. She and William had both often run late in high school, but she'd learned in the theatre world to be ready on time. She'd assumed William was still a late person, but it looked like she was wrong and he'd learned to be prompt, too.

Well, there'd be no more changes of clothes today. She glanced at her mirror. She'd already applied her makeup, and the only thing she didn't have on yet were the boots. Grabbing them and her shoulder bag, she shut her bedroom door to keep the cat out of mischief—she'd already caught him attempting to play with one of her scarves—and hurried down the stairs. "Coming," she called.

Tiger sat near the door, as if he recognized the sound of the bell and was curious about who was on the other side.

Brooke opened the door. "C'mon in," she said then paused. She'd always recognized William was a handsome guy. When she'd seen him last weekend, she'd been struck again by his good looks, but somehow, today, he looked even better. Maybe it was because he wore nice clothes, dark blue jeans and a gray slim-fitting shirt under his open leather jacket. Maybe it was because his fair hair looked as if it had just been cut.

Whatever it was, the total effect impacted her immediately. She gazed at a gorgeous guy—not a kid, but a grown man. She took a sharp breath.

He stared at her. "You look great, Brooke."

"Thanks." Was it childish to feel flattered? He stepped into the hall, and she closed the door behind him. "I'll be ready in a minute."

"Nice cat," he remarked, gazing at Tiger. Tiger responded by rubbing against William's leg.

She explained about the situation with her neighbor. "You always liked cats," she added. "Would you like to keep him?"

William looked regretful. "I would, except my roommate, Ryan, already has a cat. He rescued an old guy, and Felix—that's his name—doesn't like other cats, so I can't bring another into the house. I wouldn't do that to either of them."

"Okay. I thought I'd try," Brooke said.

"I'm planning to buy a condo eventually. Maybe I'll get a cat then," William said, reaching down to pet Tiger.

Tiger purred.

When he straightened, Brooke indicated her living room. "Make yourself comfortable." She

29

realized she'd forgotten her earrings. "I'll be down in a minute."

She dashed upstairs, grabbed the simple gold hoops she'd placed on her dresser, and put them on. After checking herself one more time in her full-length mirror, she returned downstairs to find William and Tiger sitting cozily on the couch. "How cute!"

William eased his tall body off the couch and gave Tiger a pat. "Ready to go?"

"As soon as I check his dishes." Hurrying around the counter to the kitchen, Brooke checked to make sure Tiger had plenty of water and dry food. "Okay, buddy, see you later." The cat stayed snuggled on the couch as they departed.

"I hope I find him a good home," she said, closing the door and locking it.

"You will."

They talked about the cats and dogs who were part of Brooke's family as William drove to the nearby train station. Their last dog had died several years ago, and since Brooke's parents now traveled more and there weren't any kids left at home, her parents hadn't adopted any more pets.

"My parents' house does feel funny without a dog and cat," Brooke admitted, taking a deep breath. William wore some kind of aftershave with a clean, crisp scent. She liked it.

He asked about her family, and she told him her older sister, Rebecca, practiced orthopedics with their father, was married, and expecting her first child. Her brother, Troy, was a well-known accountant, married, and had a little girl.

"And of course you've seen Jeremy," she added.

"Hey, what do you think of Nicole?" She was curious about the girl who had captured her brother's attention—and his heart, she suspected, after seeing them together last weekend.

William shot her a glance. "Nicole's really nice. She and Marla have had me over for dinner a couple of times. Nicole's a great cook and a very thoughtful person. We've never dated or anything. I kind of thought she had a boyfriend, and she's always been just a friend to me."

Brooke knew from her brother the people at the cable TV station had assumed she did have a boyfriend. It wasn't until they asked her to bring him on an episode of her show, "A Taste of Romance," that she'd had to produce an actual person and had asked Jeremy to play the part. Brooke had been amused when Jeremy confided all this, especially when she realized Jeremy was fast becoming just that, Nicole's boyfriend.

She wasn't going to share the secret, though, if William didn't know it already, so she turned the topic to what William enjoyed about his job.

"I love capturing the excitement of special features, so they can be shared with other people," he said as he stopped at a red light. "Talking to people, getting at the heart of the matter, no matter what it is, zeroing in on the important stuff. I like news stories, too, but human interest, that's my favorite. And then being able to edit the footage down, so you can get to the essence of what you want to reveal, that's the most fascinating part." He grinned as the light turned green, and they moved forward. "When you edit, you can really highlight the nuances of a subject."

"Is that what you do with the cooking show?"

He signaled and changed lanes. "With the cooking show, it's more about revealing how to do something and the beauty of what's prepared, since obviously the audience can't taste the results. You want to get them to try cooking by showing them how appealing the end product can be."

Brooke asked him questions about the editing process. Before she knew it, they were at the train station, and they didn't have to wait too long for the train. Once they were ensconced on comfortable seats William turned to face her. "So…" he drawled, "tell me about you."

Something about the way he gazed at her, his blue-gray eyes bright, his attention totally focused on her, made Brooke feel both special and peculiar, as if the world tipped off-center.

It was a strange feeling, one she wasn't used to. And she wasn't sure what caused this weird sensation. She was out for the day with an old friend. What was strange about that?

***

William regarded Brooke as she looked at him, wide-eyed. It wasn't hard to gaze at her, since she was one of the most gorgeous women he'd ever met.

She'd always turned heads. Even when she went through her most "artsy" phase and dyed her hair purple and wore strange clothes, she'd looked good. But now the pretty girl was all woman, with a slim but curvy figure in her black slacks and green sweater. Her generous smile and rosy lips were very appealing, and he wasn't surprised that a couple of guys on the train had stared at her appreciatively.

He asked her about her job, and she answered his questions readily.

"After I finished my BA and master's in scenery design, I did some freelance work," she told him. "Everywhere from Florida to Long Island. But I wanted to stay in one place, and when I heard about the opening at Quemby, I really wanted it." She paused. "I wanted to get the job on my own, too, not because I'm Sharon Maloney-Perez's child. Being my mom's daughter, I did get a few jobs, but I got plenty on my own, and I want it to stay that way."

"You always were independent," he remarked.

Brooke's blond hair swished slightly as she nodded. "I got the job, and I've been there several years now. I teach three theatre classes every semester. I'm the head of stage design for the major productions and consult with the student-run productions. And there's a small local theatre group in Warren County that has asked me to do their stage design. It's volunteer work, but I enjoy it and help out with their productions when I can."

"You sound busy." He wondered if she had much time to date.

She smiled. "You know me. I like having things to do. I do Jazzercise a few times a week, too. And I usually get together with Jeremy once a week for dinner." Before William could ask anything else, she blurted, "It's so funny you work with Nicole and got to see Jeremy!"

Yeah, funny. He'd been glad to see Jeremy—he'd always liked him—and asking Jeremy to help set up dinner so he'd see Brooke had seemed like an innocent request, in return for keeping Jeremy's famous family a secret from Nicole. Jeremy had a great desire to be liked and respected for himself, and William understood that. The whole agreement had seemed simple, at the time.

He switched the topic. "Yeah, that was quite a dinner Nicole and Marla made. I can't wait for the next one. Do you cook much?"

Brooke shook her head. "Just the basics. Although, after that meal, I'm willing to give it a try." As her head moved, he caught a whiff of her fruity cologne.

The train slowed at the next stop. William switched the topic again, asking about her condo. Brooke had bought it two years ago and liked living in Hackettstown. She asked him about the house he rented with his friend, Ryan.

Time flew so fast it seemed minutes later they pulled into the train station in New York. They were soon out on the sunny streets.

It wasn't a long walk to the galleries Brooke wanted to visit, and the weather was clear and in the sixties with a breeze, so the walk was a pleasant one. Every block or so, he caught an annoying whiff of the slight garbage smell that often popped up on the streets of the city. Fortunately, the wind kept it from becoming too oppressive.

Cars honked and buses huffed as they walked. A man on a corner, carrying a "Going out of Business" sign, yelled about rock-bottom prices.

The first gallery they reached highlighted work from an up-and-coming New Mexico artist Brooke wanted to see. She pointed out the colors, the stark play of light and shadow on the canvases, and William enjoyed not just listening to her, but watching, as well. Her brow furrowed as she studied one painting, and a little smile played around her face as she regarded another. Her slim finger pointed out the clever use of purple shadows in still another painting.

"Have you been to New Mexico?" he asked. Brooke's family had traveled a lot.

"No," she said. "But I'm thinking I'd like to go sometime."

"I've never been there, either," he said. "But I want to see New Mexico, too."

They continued to walk around. Brooke planned to buy a painting for her parents' next anniversary and took some pamphlets and information from the gallery as they left.

They walked two blocks to the next gallery on her list. This was a larger place, on the second floor of an Art-Deco style building, and the black and white tile floors and high ceilings gave it a more plush look than the first. Soft classical music played in the background, and thick curtains framed the windows.

"Thomasina West is a well-known artist from upstate New York," Brooke told him as they looked at the first piece.

It was what appeared to be a crumpled pair of shorts and two sandals, standing on a base covered in sand. The next piece was almost identical but included sunglasses and a container of lip balm. The pieces looked stiff and shiny, as if sprayed with hairspray.

William raised his brows. "This is art?"

Brooke shot him a look that was a mixture of

annoyance and amusement. "Yes, it's three-dimensional art. Don't look like that. You're an artist yourself."

"I capture moments in real life, then edit them down to get their essence," he protested.

"She's capturing moments, too," Brooke pointed out.

He wasn't convinced. They moved on to another, larger, piece.

Here were dark blue men's swimming trunks, with a red and white print bikini thrown beside them, on another sand-covered base. A tube of suntan lotion lay nearby.

"I could have done that," Will stated. "Taken one of my swim trunks, one of your swimsuits, dropped them on plastic and sprayed them."

Brooke shook her head, smiling. "It's a fun piece. It's whimsical, as if the swimmers dropped their suits in the sand and went skinny dipping."

He gave Brooke a long look, then suddenly laughed.

Brooke had always had the ability to see things in a fun and amusing way.

And he'd always liked it.

***

They visited two more galleries that afternoon, both displaying more traditional forms of art—paintings and clay sculptures. William kept joking about the odd art they'd seen with the swimsuits and other summer clothes on sand and grass-like bases. Brooke agreed it wasn't difficult to do, but disagreed that the artists had put no thought into it.

36

She suggested they eat dinner on the early side, and William agreed. They debated and settled on Tortorelli's, an Italian restaurant that was a favorite of her family's. William had eaten there before and was as enthusiastic about their food as she.

They walked briskly through the golden light of the fall afternoon, discussing the merits of the art they'd seen, with William still poking fun at the bathing suit sculptures.

"I'm telling you, I could do one of those easily," he reiterated.

The restaurant was busy, but not ridiculously so yet, and they were seated at a small table. As Brooke opened her menu, Italian music played from some nearby speakers, low so it didn't mar the conversations. People at the next table laughed, and glasses clinked. Delectable smells teased her nose.

She ordered the eggplant parmigiana, one of her favorites, and William chose the chicken cacciatore. They agreed on mushrooms stuffed with polenta and cheese as a shared appetizer.

They discussed plays they'd seen on- and off-Broadway, music concerts and rock groups they enjoyed, and the dinner sped by. Before she knew it, she was sipping coffee with William and sharing a tortoni.

"Mmm. This has been delicious," she said with a contented sigh.

"Yeah." He dipped his spoon into the creamy dessert. "I don't know what's better, this or the meal we had last week."

"They're both good," she said. "I'd get tired of restaurant food, if that was all I ate. Same with home cooking." She inhaled the aroma of the rich coffee.

"Yeah, variety is the spice of life," he joked.

Brooke excused herself to go to the ladies' room, checking her makeup, and spritzing herself with the small bottle of cologne she had in her purse. She wanted to look nice for Connie's production, she told herself. When she returned, William was just coming out of the men's room, and she noticed he had combed his hair.

They took a cab to the theatre. Once inside the cab, William slung his arm around her shoulders and without thinking, she leaned into him. Then she wondered if it was simply a friendly gesture and she shouldn't be too close. Too late—she already was.

She felt the smooth texture of his leather jacket against her face, the warmth of his neck near her forehead. As the taxi wove in and out of traffic, starting and stopping, she felt nice and cozy against his side.

The city had grown darker, but the thousands of lights made it festive as well as flashy. The theatre, situated in an old, renovated building, was small. Their seats turned out to be pretty good, ten rows back from the center stage.

The play was an amusing comedy about three musicians trying to get somewhere, early in their careers. During the intermission, Brooke sent Connie a note to say they were there and enjoying the play and they'd see her afterwards.

William didn't put his arm around her during the show, but she found herself curiously aware of him. If he switched his position or chuckled or moved his arm, she was well aware of it. This acute awareness was strange. She didn't usually feel like this with friends. Maybe with someone on a first date, but not with William—her old friend. It was odd.

They applauded at the end of the show and then went backstage.

Brooke hadn't seen Connie for several months, so she was eager to visit with her, even if it was for a short time. They had hit if off in college when they joked about Connie's parents naming her because her mom liked a certain TV anchorwoman and Brooke's parents naming her because her mom liked an actress who had been a child star. Although Brooke's mother always said she simply liked the name, she did admit she liked the actress, Brooke Shields.

Connie's husband, Ernest Wu, an architect, was already backstage, and Brooke introduced him to William after she hugged Connie and Ernie. William had met Connie before, and he shook hands with Ernie, but hugged Connie.

"The show was a lot of fun," William told them.

"The lighting was great," Brooke said. "I especially liked the way you went from bright to dark when each musician did their solos, leaving just the spotlight on them…"

They discussed the lighting as people bustled by, and they paused to congratulate some of the actors who passed near them. Connie went to supervise shutting down the lights, and Ernie excused himself to see if she needed help.

As the backstage area grew darker, William glanced around. "Reminds me of when we were in 'Bye Bye Birdie' in high school."

Brooke had had the starring role as Kim, and William had played one of the teens in town. They'd had a lot of fun working on the show together.

"This stage is smaller and spookier," Brooke told

him. She noticed a window curtain on the stage set had come loose and drooped. She didn't see any sign of the stage manager or any scenery people, but a whole group gathered by the director in the corridor, listening to some comments he made. "Here, help me with this," she said, figuring she'd rehang it herself.

There was a stepladder nearby and when she indicated it, William obligingly dragged it over. She went up a few steps and easily rehung the curtain where it sagged.

She was conscious that he was behind her, holding the ladder steadily. She put one foot down on the next step, then the other. His arms surrounded her.

Her heartrate sped up.

Brooke turned. She was much shorter than William, but on the ladder, she stood slightly above him. She inched down another step. Their eyes met at the same level.

His gaze locked on hers.

Brooke felt zapped by an electric current.

"Brooke!" Connie's voice interrupted the private moment.

William let go, and Brooke stepped down, until she reached the floor. Her head spun. The way William had looked at her, as if he wanted to kiss her…

She felt a little dazed. Because, for a moment, she had *wanted* him to kiss her.

Connie coughed.

"I…ah…fixed the curtain," Brooke said hastily. She waved in its general direction. She knew her face was flushed; she could feel the heat all over her body.

"I helped." William's voice sounded strange.

Connie pressed her lips together. Knowing her friend, Brooke guessed she probably wanted to laugh. "Thank you." The words came out solemnly, but her dark eyes twinkled.

Ernie approached. "Did you guys want to have a drink or something?"

"Ah, no," Brooke said. "We've had a long day. I think we'll head back." She glanced at William.

He met her look, then nodded. "Yeah."

"But we'll get together again soon," Brooke added, turning back to Connie. "Maybe next month?"

They hugged, and Connie whispered in Brooke's ear, "I'll call you in a couple of days."

Brooke didn't know what to say. She didn't know how she felt, except confused. William was her friend. You weren't supposed to want to kiss your friend. Were you?

She still felt somewhat dazed while they got their jackets and left the theatre.

"Want to take the subway or a cab back to the train station?" William asked as they stepped out into a brisk, cool wind.

"A subway is fine," Brooke said. The noise and bright lights should dissipate the slightly strange feeling she experienced.

The platform was crowded with people out on a Saturday night, and the subway came shortly after they got there, so there was no chance to talk amid all the noise. The ride, too, was crowded, and when they got to the train station, they discovered the next train was due to leave in twenty minutes. They discussed the play, and Brooke found herself relaxing a little as they talked about the staging and the actor's performances.

Once on the train, it was quiet, with only a few other people nearby. For the first time all day, Brooke felt awkward. They sat quietly, gazing out the window as the city lights receded and it grew dimmer outside. Brooke searched her mind for something else to say.

"I had fun today," he said first. He stretched, placed his arm around her shoulders, and pulled her closer.

"Me, too," she agreed and let her head rest on his shoulder.

He held her, lightly, not overly close, and Brooke couldn't help it when a little sigh of contentment escaped her lips.

It *had* been a lovely day. With her friend.

She tried to simply enjoy sitting close to him and not thinking. His breathing slowed, and after a few minutes, she suspected he dozed lightly.

She smiled. For a little while, she relaxed against him and enjoyed the quiet strength of his arm and shoulder.

The train's whistle roused her from semi-sleep. Brooke opened her eyes to find William's head close to hers, his lips almost touching her hair. She could still smell the faint remnants of his aftershave.

She moved slightly to view him. His eyes were open, and he was staring at her, a bemused expression on his face.

The train jarred, and the motion bumped them apart.

"I think ours is the next stop," he said, his voice slightly raspy.

"Oh." Disappointment—or was it relief?—swished inside her. "Okay." That sounded lame. "I didn't mean to doze off." She sat up.

"Me, neither." He smiled. "It was a great day."

They were wide awake and discussing the play again by the time they arrived at their station. Once he had driven her home, she asked him if he wanted coffee or a soda as he parked the car.

"I'll take a rain check," he said. "I am a little tired."

She was sad to see the evening end, but it was late. He walked her to the door, and once she'd unlocked it, he leaned down and gave her a quick kiss. "How about we talk in a few days and make some plans then?"

"Okay."

He hesitated. "Goodnight, Brooke." He smiled, then turned and went back to his car. Once there, he stopped and waved before getting in and driving away.

Brooke shut the door and locked it.

Wow.

A fun day spent with an old friend had become…what? More than friendly? Or was she reading too much into it?

But there had been that almost kiss…

She wasn't sure how she felt. Or how to handle those mixed feelings.

Tiger padded up to her from the living room, staring at her. She bent down and stroked the cat.

She was tired, too, but once in bed, she couldn't stop thinking about William. And reliving that moment when their eyes had met.

CHAPTER IV

The phone rang the following afternoon, and Brooke put aside the laundry she was folding and paused the show on TV. She'd been catching up with her mother's soap opera episodes from the week before.

"Hello?" she asked. Was it William? She hadn't glanced at the number.

"Hi, Brooke!" her sister said. "I thought I'd call and catch up with you. We haven't spoken for a while."

Brooke smiled, always glad to hear Rebecca's voice. Her older sister lived and worked in New York City. As a doctor, she was pretty busy, and since she was near the end of her pregnancy, she usually went to bed early.

"Hey! How are you feeling?" Brooke asked.

"Ugh. Heavy," Rebecca said, but her voice remained cheerful. "I feel like a roly-poly."

"Well, you look good," Brooke told her.

"Humph. You haven't seen me lately. I'm *big*! So how are you?"

They chatted for a few minutes. Brooke told her about the cat, who was sitting on the arm of the couch, half-asleep. Then she told her about William and their date.

44

"I'm a little confused," Brooke admitted.

"Why?"

"Well, I'm not sure if William is an old friend, or if something else is happening." She went on to describe their date, and how they'd had a nice, friendly time. Until she'd found herself gazing into his eyes and felt as if something had zapped her.

"Do you want it to be romantic? Or just a casual friendly relationship?"

"I thought I wanted to be friends with him," Brooke admitted with a sigh. She leaned back on the couch. "After what happened with Nate..." Rebecca was one of the few who knew about *that* disaster.

"Why did you and William break up originally?" Rebecca asked. "I was already in med school when you guys were going out."

Brooke explained that they'd dated and really liked each other. William had been the first boyfriend she'd been excited about.

"But then, I got kind of restless," she told her sister, "after a few months. We were young, and I kind of wanted to date other people, too. I had gradually fallen for William. But I kept expecting...well, that someone would come along and really sweep me off my feet. I know it sounds silly, but when you're a teenager, that's the way you think. And we had the example of Mom and Dad. I wanted that, too."

Their parents had met when Sharon, their mom, had broken her finger on the set of the soap opera. She'd gone to Antonio Perez, a young but already well-known orthopedic specialist. Their whirlwind romance had been like a fairy tale, and they were still happily married, some forty years and four children later.

Brooke had always wanted that for herself. "Didn't you want a romance like that?"

"Not really. Remember, I had that boyfriend who pursued me, and I fell for him, and then found out he just wanted to get into Dad's medical practice."

"That's right." Brooke recalled how hurt her sister had been by the betrayal, like Jeremy, who had been pursued by a woman who thought their mom would help her acting career. At least Brooke and their brother, Troy, had avoided that kind of heart-wrenching experience. "I broke up with William, although I tried to do it nicely. I convinced him we were young and should date other people. He was mad at first, but so many girls threw themselves at him he got over me pretty quick. We ended up being friends, and have been, although we haven't seen each other for a few years until now."

"Well, why not go out and have a good time?" Rebecca asked practically. "And see what happens?"

"I guess so," Brooke replied slowly.

Maybe she could.

Except the memory of their close proximity, of what could have ended up as a kiss, might make it difficult to maintain a casual relationship.

***

Brooke watched from the sidelines as the guest lecturer on stage concluded his speech about King Tut and Egyptian mummies.

He clicked his remote control, and the screen behind him showed a golden sarcophagus. "You can see why this was considered such an important find," he said, waving his hand with a flourish.

He was an interesting speaker, Brooke thought, full of unusual facts and research, with an enthusiastic way of speaking. A professor at an Ivy League university, who had done archaeological digs, written academic papers, and popular books, Derek Sims was a good-looking man in his mid-thirties.

Each semester, Quemby College brought in guest lecturers on different topics. The lectures were free to students and open to the immediate community for a nominal fee. The theatre was pretty full this Wednesday evening, probably because the topic of Egyptian mummies was so popular, and also because Derek Sims was a well-known name. Brooke had volunteered to help backstage at this particular lecture because she found the topic fascinating. The speaker himself appeared equally fascinating.

He finished his remarks to loud applause. The history professor who had introduced Sims said they had time for a few questions, and he would be signing his latest book in the mezzanine shortly after the lecture.

From her vantage point backstage, Brooke saw hands raised immediately. A lot of the listeners appeared to be Quemby students, but plenty of other people, from middle-aged to senior citizens, sat in the audience, as well.

The question and answer period ended after ten minutes, and Derek Sims stepped back as applause sounded once more.

"Okay," Brooke said into her microphone to Geraldo, the student in charge of lights tonight. "You can turn off the spotlight and start shutting down in two minutes." The lights back here were dim, and she wanted to make sure the guest speaker could see as he made his way off the stage.

The curtains rustled, and she heard a muffled, "Oof!" before Derek Sims thrust aside the curtain and appeared near the pulley.

"Are you all right?" she asked, moving towards him.

"Yes, I should have watched where I was going. I almost hit myself in the face with the curtain," he said cheerfully.

"That was a fascinating lecture."

He smiled and responded, "I'm glad you thought so," in his appealing, masculine voice.

"I did," she said. "I'll have to get your book when I'm finished back here."

He appeared to study her.

"Brooke, right?" They had been introduced briefly before his lecture started, and she was impressed when he remembered her name. "You know, I have a short interview to do and then the books to sign. Do you want to meet up for a drink afterwards?"

His suggestion took her by surprise, as did the flirtatious look on his face.

Hmm…drinks with Derek Sims? He was good-looking and seemed personable.

But she was cautious. She had only met this guy for a few minutes and wasn't sure she wanted to go to a pub or bar with him.

"I have an early day tomorrow," she said. "But I could meet you at the Coffee House for a quick snack." That was a place a few blocks from the college, where students and teachers could often be found.

He wrinkled his nose slightly. "Well, if that's my only choice. I guess that's okay. I know where it is. I've been around here before. Let's see, it's..." He glanced at his watch. "Just after 8:30. Suppose I meet you there in forty-five minutes?"

"That's fine," Brooke said.

"And I'll bring you a book," he offered.

"That's okay. I'll buy one."

There was a loud click as Geraldo shut down the largest light.

"That was wonderful!" Professor Bridges, the woman who taught several ancient history classes and who had introduced the speaker, appeared behind him. "Now, we must get you out to meet all the people who want to buy autographed books."

"Okay," he said, winking at Brooke.

"And don't forget, there's a reporter here form Morris Cable," the professor said, leading the way past curtains and equipment to the stage door.

Brooke made sure the projection screen was retracted and the student helper had removed the equipment Derek had needed. She finished checking to see everything was in place, and then exited herself.

In the corridor, she stopped short.

An established woman reporter Brooke recognized held a mic out to Derek, asking him about a new theory on King Tut's reign. Standing nearby, videotaping, was William.

Unexpectedly, her heart thumped. `

William didn't seem to notice her at first. He moved slightly, changing the camera's angle, as Derek replied to the reporter's question. He appeared to zero in on Derek's face.

Brooke listened to Derek's pleasant voice, expounding on the theory, but also questioning some aspects, leaving the reporter with, "So, we still have a lot more research to do into the life of King Tut; in fact, there are a lot of questions still to be answered about all the pharaohs." He beamed at the camera.

"Thank you," the reporter said. She smiled at the camera as William swung it around to focus on her face. "And this is Kathleen Murray with Morris Cable. We'll bring you more information on the lectures at Quemby College, and others, as they occur." She paused.

"That's a wrap," William declared.

"Over here," Lillian Bridges said, guiding Derek towards the front of the theatre. "Your fans are waiting!"

Derek turned slightly. He met Brooke's eyes and gave her a wide smile. "See you later."

Brooke returned his smile, then watched as he followed the professor, and the reporter began winding the cord of her mic.

William lowered his camera and turned to stare at Brooke.

"Hi, William," she greeted him, feeling a little awkward. How much did he read into Derek's casual comment?

And why was she concerned?

***

Derek was ten minutes late for coffee.

While she waited, Brooke played with her iPhone, texting Connie, checking emails and looking

50

at the weather app. She replayed her meeting with William in her mind. He'd seemed cool and business-like when she saw him. They'd spoken for only a couple of minutes, despite the fun they'd had on Saturday.

Was he feeling awkward about their time together?

Or was it that she'd caught him by surprise while he was working? Perhaps, he was so wrapped up in his job at that moment he wasn't inclined to socialize. She understood that. She often got so involved in her work she didn't want any distractions. Or maybe he needed to get back to the studio right away and edit the footage for the next morning's news.

They'd spoken on the phone on Monday, but he'd worked late and couldn't talk for long. Now, she wondered if that was true or if he'd been feeling strange.

William had always been honest with her. No, he probably did have to work late on Monday.

She sighed and turned her attention to thoughts of Derek. He was handsome, personable, the kind to make a woman's heart beat faster. She wondered if he was like the movie character, archaeologist Indiana Jones, and had lots of women after him. Probably! But then, Derek did look like a romantic hero.

"Sorry I'm late." He strode up to her table and placed his laptop case on it, giving her a winning smile.

The Coffee House was crowded, both with students and people who'd probably attended his lecture. Brooke recognized a few of the history professors from the college, plus two music professors she knew, sitting at nearby tables.

They ordered, with Derek choosing coffee and a piece of chocolate cake. Brooke chose hot chocolate, since the night had turned cold for early October. He paid for them both, and they brought their food back to their table.

"How'd the book sale go?" she asked.

Derek spoke about the book sale and his tour. He'd reduced his class load to one class this semester so he could promote his new book, he told her. The college where he taught was cooperative, since he got them a lot of national attention.

"I'll be going back to Egypt for more research for the entire month of January, so I have to prepare for that, too," he said.

Brooke found him interesting and amusing, and she asked him a few questions about how he'd gotten into Egyptology.

"I was fascinated by mummies since I was about seven and saw an Egyptian exhibit in a museum. My parents are historians, too. Both are professors, my mom specializing in medieval studies, and my dad in colonial America. Both teach at a large university in New York state, so it was natural for me to go this route." He leaned forward. "Now tell me about you." His voice dropped to a husky note.

Brooke told him a little about herself, eliminating any reference to her famous family. Although she kept telling her brother he should be up front with Nicole and tell the truth about the famous Perez family, Brooke didn't feel obligated to spill all on a first date.

Or kind-of-a-date.

Derek smiled and glanced at his watch. "Well, I have over an hour's drive back to my condo. I better get going." He sounded reluctant. "Can you give me your phone number? I'd like to get together with you soon."

Brooke dictated her number, and he programmed it into his iPhone. They stood up, and he gallantly helped her on with her jacket.

Definitely hero material, Brooke thought as they walked together outside.

"Where's your car?" he asked.

The night air was cold and clear, and a sprinkling of stars, plus a partial moon, shone down on them. Brooke took a deep breath of the fresh autumn air and pointed to her car, parked across the lot.

He walked with her, and after she pushed the clicker to unlock the door, she turned to him. "Thanks, Derek. I'm looking forward to reading the book."

"Hope you enjoy it." He leaned down, and unexpectedly, gave her a quick kiss on the lips. His lips were warm on hers. "I'll call you soon."

Once inside her car, Brooke started it and turned on the lights. After snapping on her seatbelt, she sat there for a moment.

She touched her lips with one finger. Derek had kissed her after only knowing her a few hours. Not that this hadn't happened with other guys before, but...

The night had taken on a colorful hue.

Had she met a romantic hero?

Well, she certainly wouldn't trust him until she did a little research on Professor Derek Sims.

***

"What's up, buddy?"

Will looked up from closing the oven door to see his roommate, Ryan, standing in the kitchen doorway. He placed the frozen pizza he'd heated on the top of the stove, turned off the oven, and threw down the potholder. "I'm hungry. Want some?" he asked, indicating the pizza.

"Yeah, I'll have a slice."

Will grabbed a couple of paper plates and slammed the cabinet door.

"Are you okay?" Ryan asked, selecting a slice and placing it on the plate Will handed him. "I could hear you rattling around in here from my bedroom."

It was just past eleven, and Will had come home a short time ago, after returning to the cable studio for some preliminary editing of the footage on Derek Sims and his Egyptology presentation and interview.

He tried to edit it fairly and not cut it down to bare, boring minimum, which was what he really wanted to do, so Derek wasn't seen in the best light. But, of course, that would be unprofessional. He'd forced himself not to get emotional.

Will sighed loudly and sat at the kitchen table across from Ryan, who had brought out a couple of beers from the refrigerator.

"I ran into Brooke tonight at that Egyptology talk I was covering," Will said. He bit into the pizza. It was a brand he normally liked a lot, but somehow tonight the tomato sauce, cheese and sausage had little taste.

"And...?" Ryan prompted.

"And she was talking to Derek, the speaker. A lot. He was hitting on her." Will frowned. In the background, the radio played AC/DC. It suited his mood.

"Hmph." Ryan chewed for a moment. Ryan worked in Human Resources for a large corporation nearby. They'd been friends in college, and once they'd learned they were working at companies close by each other, they'd rented a house together. The house was big enough so they each had their own space and didn't get in each other's way, yet they could hang out and spend time together when they wanted to, like right now.

"How did you feel about that?" Ryan asked after a moment.

That was easy. "Annoyed. Angry."

Ryan nodded. "What do you think you should do?"

Yesterday, over dinner at a local diner, Will had told Ryan he'd enjoyed the day he'd spent with Brooke in the city. He didn't talk about the fact he'd been tempted to kiss her, but he had confided he wanted to see her again.

"I don't know," he admitted now.

"Maybe this is a good time to make your own move," Ryan suggested.

"My own move?"

"Sure." Ryan took a swig of beer. "Let her know you're interested in her as a girlfriend, not just a friend. That you like her the same way this guy does. She may be thinking he's the only one who's attracted to her in that way."

Will took another bite of pizza, chewing thoughtfully. The singer on the radio shrieked about being back in black. "You think? Like, how?"

Ryan shrugged. "You could show up with flowers. Liz loves it when I bring her flowers."

"She might like something different. She's very artistic," Will pointed out.

"Flowers in an artistic vase?"

55

Will grinned. The pizza was tasting better. "I'll give it some thought."

They tossed around some ideas, like DVDs of funny TV shows, candy, an afternoon at a museum.

"But we went to a play and spent the afternoon at some galleries," Will said.

"Jewelry is always a hit," Ryan said, "though expensive."

Will nodded. "She likes to wear interesting earrings." She'd had a pair on tonight that had clear-colored stones in the shape of small stars.

"That's it. Think of a small gift she'd like," Ryan said. "And ask her out for a nice dinner or something."

Of course, they'd already gone out for dinner. But it was worth a try.

"Maybe I'll call her and suggest we go out this weekend," he said.

Later, as he was getting ready to sleep, he decided Ryan was right. He'd call Brooke, invite her out for dinner, and then maybe find something to bring her. Something small, just to show he was thinking of her.

But when he closed his eyes, he saw Derek Sims, smiling flirtatiously at Brooke.

He'd like to smack that grin right off the professor's smug face.

CHAPTER V

On Thursday, Brooke entered her office after class, placed her laptop case and tote bag on her desk, and turned on her cellphone.

Shrugging out of her jacket, she sat at her desk. She had the office to herself at the moment, and the ping of her phone echoed in the room, letting her know she had voicemail.

The first message was from Adrielle, saying she'd found a new antique store in Hackettstown that could be a source of future props. "And their prices seem reasonable," she'd added. "It's close to the other antique stores and not far from the thrift shop where I've picked up a few things."

The second one was from Derek.

"I had a good time last night," he said. "Listen, I have to go to Boston on Saturday because I'm giving a couple of lectures up there starting on Sunday. How about we get together Friday night? There's a new performance of *Macbeth* in Princeton that sounds interesting."

She'd heard about the production, which featured some up-and-coming actors, and it did sound interesting. She'd have to call him back.

Almost the minute she'd reached home last night, she'd gone on the internet and researched Professor Derek Sims.

She was relieved to find out he was single. No hidden wives he'd concealed, no surprises. Two popular online entertainment and pop culture sites said he'd broken his engagement last year, but nothing further. Apparently his ex-fiancé had been a well-known archaeologist, too.

The third message on her phone was from William.

"Hi, Brooke," he said. "I'd really like to get together with you this weekend. I know we're having supper with everybody on Sunday. How about if we go out on Saturday night? Maybe for Chinese food, since we had Italian last time?"

Well. That should work out nicely.

Brooke grinned and texted Adrielle she'd received her message.

The office door opened. "You look like the Cheshire Cat in 'Alice in Wonderland,'" Bernie said, striding in.

"Oh, just having a good day," Brooke said lightly.

She didn't want Bernie, or anyone, to hear her conversations, so she decided to call both Derek and William back later, when she was alone. She got to work looking over her plans for the next set of classes, then began correcting papers she'd collected.

Bernie left an hour later.

She called Derek first, only because he'd called her first. Derek lived near the theatre he'd mentioned, so she agreed to meet him there, since he had a lot of driving to do the following day.

When she reached William, he suggested they go to a Chinese restaurant not far from where she lived, which he'd heard was good. Brooke had been there many times and loved their food, so she agreed.

It looked like it would be a very interesting weekend. Friday with Derek, Saturday and Sunday with William.

***

Brooke had been to this theatre before, and when she pulled into the parking lot she saw Derek exiting his car, a new-looking red Range Rover.

"Thanks for meeting me here," he said when she approached him.

"No problem." He looked handsome in his sports jacket, dark blue shirt and bright yellow and blue tie.

They entered the lobby, which was filled with well-dressed people.

"You look fantastic," Derek said, his eyes sweeping over her.

"Thanks." She had chosen to wear a charcoal gray knit dress, knee-high black boots, and a gray, blue and green scarf along with long earrings with lapis stones. She'd wanted to dress fashionably. Normally, she didn't mind being the center of attention—she did enjoy being on the stage—but he was studying her so openly it was a trifle uncomfortable. "Why don't we find our seats?"

They chatted for a few minutes about the series of lectures he was going to do, and then the lights dimmed.

She'd always enjoyed Shakespeare, and the

performance of *Macbeth* was a good one. As usual, she paid careful attention to the staging and during the intermission, scribbled some observations on the small pad of paper she always kept in her purse.

"Taking notes?" Derek asked.

"Yes, I always make note of new and interesting staging ideas. You never know when I can use one in the future," she told him, sliding her paper and pen back into her purse.

"I see. You know, I did a little research on you last night on the internet."

You're not the only one who did research. She raised her eyebrows. "Oh?"

"Yes." He grinned. "You're modest. I see you're well-known in your field."

"Yes." She couldn't help being pleased at his comment.

"And you come from a pretty famous family."

Oh, no, don't go *there*, she thought. She said, in a matter-of-fact voice, "Yes." And left it at that.

He asked her a few questions. He seemed impressed by her family, something she didn't care for. She didn't want to share Jeremy's and Rebecca's experiences.

She was having divided thoughts about Derek. As the lights dimmed for the next act, she considered them. On one hand, he was personable, interesting, and good-looking. On the other, he was a little too smooth, and perhaps a little too impressed by her family.

She'd have to see what happened.

After the show, they went to a restaurant within walking distance of the theatre for dessert. They discussed the show, and Derek asked about what she thought of the staging and scenery.

"The special effects for the witches were excellent," Brooke said as she was served a piece of apple pie. "And the lightning around Lady Macbeth was very atmospheric."

When he walked her back to her car, he promised to call when he returned from Massachusetts.

"I'd like to see you again," he said, and, placing his hands on her shoulders, swooped down to give her a kiss.

As a kiss, it wasn't bad. Brooke waited, expecting to feel her heart leap.

But while her heart did beat a tad quicker, she didn't feel the giant fluttering she'd expected.

Oh, well. It was only their first—no, second—date.

But on the way home, she found herself thinking, not so much about Derek, but about her date with William tomorrow.

***

"There." Jeremy stepped back and wiped his hands on an old towel. "That's fixed."

"Thanks, Bro!" Brooke gave Jeremy a quick hug. They stood on the stage, near a light that kept going out. Jeremy had found a problem with the connection and fixed it. "Just give me an invoice, and I'll make sure the college pays you right away."

"Good job," Geraldo said, turning it on again. "This should do it. Thanks!"

"Want a soda or something?" she asked, glancing at her watch. It was just after three on Saturday.

61

Jeremy shook his head. "Sorry. I have to stop at a house and check an electrical problem they're having. But I'll see you tomorrow."

Originally they'd had plans to have dinner again with Nicole, William, Marla and Scott. But their dad had called early this morning, offering them six tickets to a Giants football game on Sunday. Someone had given them to him at the last minute, and he'd thought perhaps Brooke and Jeremy could use them, since he and their mom were attending a wedding. They were excited at the prospect. Brooke had called Nicole and the dinner plans had rapidly changed to brunch before the football game.

"Okay," she said to her brother. "See you tomorrow."

After Jeremy departed, she and Geraldo locked up the theatre. Brooke was starting her car when her cellphone rang.

William's name came up on the display. "Hi." She wondered why her voice came out so breathlessly.

"Hi, Brooke. Listen, I have to work later than expected. Ben--one of the other cameramen--his wife went into labor early, and they asked me to cover the health fair at the county college after I finished taping the home improvement show. I'm here at the health fair now, which means I'll be late."

"Oh, that's okay," she said. She certainly understood that things came up at work and, like her, William had to work some weekends.

"I think I'll be back at the studio, and we'll have things wrapped up, by seven," he said. "Why don't I call you when I'm on my way?"

"That's fine," she said. She was glad he hadn't cancelled. "Maybe we should just bring the Chinese food in and eat here."

"That's a good idea," he said. "Okay, I better go. Talk to you later."

"Bye," she said and clicked off.

She didn't mind if they ate at her home. At least they'd be spending a relaxing evening together. Maybe they could watch a DVD. She had a pretty good collection.

Once home, she took a quick shower to wash away the dust from backstage, and changed from her old jeans and sweatshirt to newer jeans and a pale blue top. She played with Tiger for a while before he yawned and settled down in one of his favorite spots, the corner of her couch.

She glanced at her watch. It would be several hours until William was here. She had a granola bar so she wouldn't be starving, and settled down to watch another episode of her mom's show.

Her mom was in a lot of scenes, so she found it especially enjoyable. When the episode ended, she got up and emailed her mother to tell her how much she'd enjoyed it and what a good job she'd done.

She checked her new email, which included a joke from Rebecca and a note from Connie. After emailing them, she looked at her watch. 6:15. Hopefully, she'd hear from William soon. She then took out a notebook and glanced at notes she'd made a few weeks ago for the community theatre's production of *The Mikado*. She was doing the scenery for the show and would be talking to the director later that week.

It was actually seven forty-five before she heard from William. She'd given into hunger and had a small grilled cheese sandwich and watched the final episode of her mom's show for the week.

"I'm sorry," he apologized the moment she picked up the phone. "We took longer than I expected. I'm on my way now."

Brooke suggested she pick up the food, but he insisted. Forty minutes later, he rang her doorbell.

"You must be starved," she said as he entered her home. She noticed he looked tired. "Here, I'll take the food. I put out some sodas."

Brooke wasn't sure if it was the smell of food or curiosity to see William that had Tiger hurrying over to join them in the dining area.

"Hi, Tiger." William bent to scratch the cat. Straightening, he reached for his chicken with cashews.

Brooke scooped fried rice onto her plate and passed it to him. "Here. Want some of my chow mein?"

As they ate, William talked about the health fair, which had included massage demonstrations, exercise equipment, appliances to make your own juice, and a plethora of other related services.

Brooke enjoyed listening to him. She couldn't help noticing how comfortable it felt, like old, familiar friends.

"The best thing we got on tape," he said, pausing to sip a cola, "was a psychologist who uses laughter to help people relieve stress. He was wearing funny eyeglasses and a weird tie. We did an interview with him, and he had some great things to say about humor helping people to live healthier lives."

"I believe that," she said, taking another helping of chow mein. "I'd love to see the footage."

"They're going to run it on Monday," he told her.

Once they'd finished their dinners, they broke open their fortune cookies. "'Your life will be full of color,'" Brooke read, and laughed. "That's a good fortune."

"Especially for someone artistic like you," William said. He studied his. "'Good fortune is coming your way.'"

"That's great."

She suggested they watch one of her DVDs, and after debating a few titles, they settled on an action-adventure movie. They cleaned up dinner, brought their sodas into the living room, and settled down to watch.

They sat companionably close, and after a few minutes, William moved closer and put his arm around her.

Now, she wondered if this was more like a date than dinner with a friend. She couldn't help feeling warm and cozy next to William. She was also acutely aware of him—the woodsy scent of his aftershave, the tickle of his breath on her scalp. Without thinking, she snuggled closer.

The movie was good, but not the most suspenseful, and it began to get a little far-fetched. Still, she enjoyed it.

About two-thirds of the way through, William gave a sudden snore.

Brooke turned to look at him. His eyes were closed, his head bent down, his face relaxed and peaceful. He'd fallen asleep.

She sighed, repositioning herself. He'd put in a long day and was obviously tired. Oh, well. At least he'd still wanted to spend the evening with her.

Tiger leaped on the couch beside her and purred, almost in unison with William's breathing.

Brooke settled in to watch the rest of the movie. Even the climactic scene with cars racing and people shooting didn't wake him.

When the credits rolled and the music blared, he opened his eyes. "Is it over?" he asked sleepily.

"Yes. You fell asleep."

A look of consternation flashed across his face. "Oh. I'm sorry!"

"It's okay," she reassured him. "You must be beat."

He sat straight up and let go of her, scrubbing his hands over his face. "Yeah, I am. I guess I better go home. We have an early day tomorrow, and I promised I'd pick up some juice and paper goods for brunch."

"Will you be okay to drive?" He still looked fatigued.

"Yes. I wish…"

She waited for him to continue.

"I wish…I wasn't so tired. We barely got to spend time together."

"We will tomorrow," she assured him.

She gave him some of the Chinese food to take home and eat later in the week. At the door, he turned back to her. "I'll pick you up tomorrow morning," he said. "G'night, Brooke." He bent forward and gave her a gentle kiss.

But even that small kiss had her heart beating harder.

After William left, Brooke felt restless. It was after eleven, and although it had been a full day, she wasn't tired enough to sleep yet. She didn't want to watch any more TV, so she got into her pajamas and grabbed the mystery novel she'd started to read last week. It was a funny mystery, and she read for a while until she felt sleepy, then switched off the light.

She didn't want to think about William, or Derek, or Nate. She deliberately turned her thoughts to some possible shows they could consider doing during the spring semester at the college. They often did musicals, and "Bye Bye Birdie" popped into her head. That was such a fun show. She'd loved being part of it in high school and sharing the experience with William.

Just before she fell asleep, his smiling face drifted through her mind.

***

Brunch was delicious, and Brooke enjoyed the camaraderie around Nicole and Marla's table.

William seemed well-rested, and they drove to the stadium together. The game turned out to be an exciting one. As she sat beside him, yelling every time the Giants made a touchdown and groaning when they fumbled, she stole looks at him periodically.

He was enthusiastic and managed to converse with everyone there. Brooke found herself wondering. Did he like her as a friend? Or, did he feel something more? So far, there'd been no indication she was anything but a friend to him, which, she reminded herself, was just the way she wanted it.

At one point, Nicole and Jeremy went to get snacks, and Nicole came back, looking perturbed. She told Brooke Jeremy had run into a friend. Curious, Brooke got up to see what was what, and get a few minutes alone with her brother.

Jeremy admitted he still hadn't told Nicole about their famous family and had been afraid his friend would blurt out something.

Brooke scolded him—big sister, good-natured scolding, and he reiterated he would tell Nicole. Soon.

Brooke sighed, hoping Nicole wouldn't be too upset when she found out the truth and that Jeremy had kept it hidden from her.

While returning to her seat, she felt some sympathy for Nicole. She would be upset if William— correction, if anyone—kept secrets from her.

After the game, Brooke suggested she and William visit friends who lived not too far away from the Meadowlands. Stacy had gone to high school with them. She'd married a guy who graduated a year before they all had, but her husband had grown up around the corner from William's house. William knew him and readily agreed.

Once they arrived at Stacy and Zach's house, they sat and discussed football over pizza until Stacy changed the topic.

"Did you guys hear about Sam?" Stacy asked, handing Brooke a slice.

"What about him?" Brooke asked. Sam had been their class vice-president.

"He got arrested," Zach said, "last week."

"Really?" asked William, taking the piece of pepperoni pizza Zach handed him. "Why?"

"Well, he and his wife—I don't remember her name—opened a spa about two years ago in town," Stacy said. "She ran the hands-on part, the beauty treatments and stuff. Sam was in charge of the bookkeeping, accounting, advertisements, the business end. Supposedly they were doing well. They had fancy cars, European vacations, you name it."

"And?" Brooke asked.

"Well, she must have grown suspicious of something," Stacy said. "Because she brought in an accountant, and it turned out large sums of money were missing. Sam had lied to her all along. He was spending the money the spa made on himself and not paying the bills."

"They got shut down," Zach added.

"How awful!" Brooke exclaimed.

"That's terrible. And I always thought he was a good class vice-president," William remarked.

Brooke shook her head. "Everyone liked him. I remember thinking he was an honest guy back in high school."

"I know," Stacy concurred. "But look at him now."

"A cheat, an embezzler, and a liar," Brooke said. "Humph. What a jerk!"

She noticed William staring at her.

"Yeah," he agreed.

He looked a trifle pale.

Had William known Sam better than she thought? He definitely looked upset about what Sam had done.

***

Promising to see Stacy and Zach again soon, William and Brooke left their friends' home and went out into the cool evening air. Darkness was falling earlier and earlier, and it definitely felt like autumn.

Will liked the fall season, with its cool, clear

evenings and football, basketball and hockey games. Not to mention skiing would start in a couple of months—sometimes sooner, if they got an early snow up in Sussex County.

As he and Brooke headed west, he snapped on the radio to a rock station, and she leaned back.

"That was fun," she said lightly. "I'm glad we got to see them."

"Yeah," he agreed, wondering if she was going to bring up the topic of Sam, the class vice president-turned-embezzler. He hoped she didn't.

She did.

"Isn't that something about Sam?" It was clear from her words and tone she was disgusted by the actions of their former classmate.

And while he certainly had never done anything like Sam—and he never would—he *had* lied to Brooke. He'd arranged his reunion with her and hadn't admitted it.

What would she say when he told her the truth?

He was tempted to tell her now and get it over with.

"Nicole seems to be a very warm person," she said, changing the topic. Will went along with the new subject. She hadn't asked too many questions the last time they'd discussed Nicole, and it seemed Brooke wanted to know more about her. "How long have you known her?" she asked. "What do you think of her?"

"She's had the show a little less than a year, so I haven't known her very long," Will said. "But I like her."

She was silent for a moment. "Did you ever think about dating her?"

70

He made a left turn on the road leading to the interstate. "No. When I met her, I thought she had a boyfriend, and I didn't want to get involved in any triangles. It wasn't 'til Jeremy came on the show that I realized she didn't. She told me Jeremy was acting the part of her boyfriend, but asked me not to say anything to anyone else." He hesitated, and sent Brooke a glance. She was staring straight ahead.

Did she wonder if he would have gone for Nicole, if he'd known she didn't have a boyfriend? "I like Nicole as a friend. Period." He glanced at Brooke again. He'd said as much before, but he sensed she wanted to hear it again.

She seemed to relax against the seat. "I like her, too."

He wanted to reach over and squeeze her hand. He lifted his from the steering wheel, when suddenly a truck passed them, going fast. He was forced to grip the steering wheel. The truck blared its horn at a car in front of it. The car pulled in front of Will, nearly cutting him off, and he had to slow down. As the car swerved, the truck passed that car, too.

Will muttered under his breath.

"Well, he looks like he's in a hurry to go somewhere," Brooke said. "Anyway, I do like Nicole, and I think she's good for Jeremy. I haven't seen him this happy in…well, in ages. Not that he isn't normally happy. I mean, happy with a girlfriend."

"Your brother is a good guy. I'm glad he's happy too." Rain misted the windshield, and he paid careful attention to the road, on the lookout for more crazy drivers.

"Thanks."

They were silent for a few minutes, and once again, he was tempted to reach out and squeeze Brooke's hand, when he heard music.

"Oh, that's my cell phone," she said and dug in her purse. She lifted out her iPhone and glanced at it. The dim light illuminated the dark car. She pursed her lips and put it away. "It's a friend. I'll call them back later."

Them? Not him or her? Will's gut twisted. It had to be that Egyptian expert, Derek, calling. He gritted his teeth.

Brooke began talking about the game, and he followed her lead. But all the while, as he drove, he wondered about Brooke's interest in Derek.

The guy was just *too* smooth, too sophisticated. Couldn't Brooke see that?

Or was that something she liked?

They reached her place, and after he parked the car, she invited him to come in for a soda. His cellphone rang as they approached her door.

He was tempted to ignore it, but decided to take a quick look at the number, like Brooke had.

Maybe it would be some woman who was interested in him. Then he mentally grimaced at his childish thoughts. He had no way of knowing for sure if Derek had called her earlier. And he sure wasn't about to ask.

He peered at his phone. "It's my boss."

"Go ahead and take it," Brooke urged. She unlocked the door, her keys jangling.

"Joe?" Will said. There must be an emergency at the station for Joe to call him on a Sunday night. Brooke had left a light on in the living room, and now she turned on lights in the hall and kitchen as she walked through the condo. Will stayed in the hall.

"Hi, Will, I was wondering if you can do me a favor. You're not scheduled to work tomorrow until noon, but with Ben out because of his new baby, we're juggling schedules here. Instead of working noon until eight, can you do nine to five? I can get someone to cover the twelve to eight slot."

Will tried to be flexible when he could, and it didn't matter to him what Monday's schedule was. "Yeah, I can do that."

Tiger appeared from the shadows and wound around Will's ankles, letting out a deep purr.

"Great. Great. I really appreciate this, Will."

After they ended the conversation, William moved towards the kitchen.

Brooke had shed her jacket and poured sodas for them both. "Problems at work?"

Will explained about his boss juggling everyone's schedules and that he had to go in earlier than he'd planned. He drank some soda, then set it down on the counter. "I better get going," he told her reluctantly. "I'll have to get up early tomorrow."

"Okay," she said. Will wondered if she was eager to call that guy back. *If* it was Derek. Which, he admitted to himself, was something he didn't know.

He felt like growling in frustration and forced himself not to say anything.

Brooke walked him to the front door, where he hesitated.

"I'll call you in a couple of days," he promised. "Maybe we can get together next weekend?"

"I'd like that," she replied.

He bent and gave her a quick kiss, wishing he had more time to take her in his arms and really kiss her.

But even if he did, he felt awkward about the whole phone call that was possibly from Derek.

"Goodnight," she said softly.

"Goodnight." He left, thrusting his hands in his pockets.

That short kiss had him feeling warm all over.

CHAPTER VI

Brooke set aside Derek's book and turned off the light. The topic was fascinating, but if she didn't go to sleep soon, she'd have trouble getting up in the morning. But thoughts whirling around in her mind kept her awake.

William had seemed so casual today. Like a friend. And wasn't that *exactly* what she wanted?

When they'd arrived at her home, he'd seemed distant. She wondered if something was on his mind.

Maybe he didn't enjoy spending time with her?

She felt a pang deep within. She enjoyed his company—a lot. The idea he might not feel the same hurt. She really wanted his friendship. And she could really use a male friend.

She switched her position, clutching her pillow.

And what about Derek?

The phone call she'd received while in the car was from Derek. After William left, she'd listened to his message.

"Hi, Brooke," he'd said. "I had expected to be home by Thursday and hoped we could get together next weekend. But I've been asked to give a talk at a museum in Chicago, filling in for someone who's in the hospital, so I'm flying out on Friday. I'll call you in a couple of days, and maybe we can figure out something for the weekend after."

It was nice Derek had been thoughtful enough to call. She wasn't overly disappointed she wouldn't see him next weekend. She hardly knew him, and although she enjoyed his company, she felt rather cautious about spending much time with him.

She sighed. She really needed to get to sleep. Turning over again, she forced herself to think about something soothing, the brunch they'd had that morning.

She fell asleep to the sound of quiet rain and had a mostly restful night until she dreamed of Egyptian mummies running around on stage at Quemby College, and William videotaping them. Nicole served food for them all, while Jeremy sat at a table in the corner, sampling some of the tidbits.

Her alarm went off, interrupting the weird dream.

Brooke sat up in bed. Sunshine peeked around the shades in her bedroom. It was 7:30, and a noise made her look down. Tiger sat near one side of her bed, looking up at her.

"Good morning to you, too." He hopped over her pink slippers, walking into the hall with another funny noise—not quite a yowl, not quite a grunt—as if telling her to hurry up and give him breakfast. "I'm coming," she told him and laughed. Now, she was talking to a cat!

***

After attending a Jazzercise class with her friend Kelly, Brooke went home, showered, and ate dinner.

She'd shared her rather mixed feelings about Derek and William with Kelly, a music professor at Quemby. Brooke settled at her desk to finish grading papers, with Tiger curled up on the chair in her home office, when her cellphone sounded. The tune was "Walk Like an Egyptian," which she'd programmed for Derek's number.

"Hey, Brooke!"

They chatted about the guest lectures he'd given in the last few days, and he told her he wasn't sure when he'd be back in New Jersey. "Possibly not until next Monday or Tuesday," he said. "Good thing they're giving me a lot of time off from the university this semester to do all these book promotions and guest lectures."

Before Brooke could say anything further, he said, "There's my call waiting. I'll call you later this week. Bye." He got off the phone abruptly.

Brooke disconnected, too.

Tiger looked at her curiously.

"He didn't even ask how *I* am," she said, annoyed.

Tiger meowed in sympathy.

Brooke didn't hear from William until the following evening when she was driving back from a rehearsal at the Quemby Mountain College Theatre. The theatre group for education majors at Quemby was putting on a show.

Her phone rang with "You've Got a Friend," the ring she'd assigned to William, and she smiled and continued the drive home. Once home and ensconced on her sofa, she called him back.

"Hey, Brooke. I missed you."

He missed her? That was interesting.

Tiger jumped up on her lap, turned in a circle, plopped down, and purred loudly.

She stroked the cat as they spoke, keeping her tone neutral. "I was thinking about you, too."

"That's good. I was wondering if you'd like to go out to dinner on Saturday. I was thinking someplace nice, like the Black Horse Inn, to make up for last Saturday."

"Oh, you don't have to take me any place fancy," she blurted, then reconsidered. *Why am I saying that? Even if he is a friend, it might be nice to go someplace posh with him.*

"No, I want to. We brought in food last week, and I ended up falling asleep, so this week we'll do something nicer."

"Okay, but I did enjoy the evening with you anyway, despite your falling asleep," she said, a teasing note in her voice.

Tiger blinked.

He chuckled. "Thanks. How's six o'clock?"

She went over her plans for Saturday. "I'm helping backstage for the educational children's production Saturday. There's a performance from one to two-thirty, and then again from four to five-thirty. They've had scenery problems and asked me to stick around to help. We could meet at the theatre," she suggested.

He hesitated a moment. "That's okay, but what about your car? I'd rather drive with you than take two cars to the restaurant. Unless we pick up yours later."

That would mean she'd have to drive home by herself. She hadn't minded doing it with Derek, but right now, she felt she wanted to spend time with

William. "I think I can get someone to drive me to the college. I can ask Rita for a ride. She lives only a few minutes from here." Rita was a part-time instructor at Quemby, who taught a course in Creative Drama for Children and was one of the people in charge of the performance.

"Sounds good," he said.

They spoke for another couple of minutes until he had to get back to editing footage he'd taken that afternoon, so they agreed to meet at about six, when the play was over and her obligations were done.

She smiled as they ended the call.

Tiger purred again.

***

William propped his feet up on the worn coffee table and listened as Jeremy's phone rang.

"Hello," Jeremy answered.

"Hey, Jer," William said. "It's me, William." It was still early enough that he figured Jeremy was probably home too, relaxing.

"Hey. How are you?"

They exchanged pleasantries, then William got to the point. "Did you ever tell Nicole about your family?" He figured, if Jeremy had spilled the beans, he should probably tell Brooke how he'd maneuvered meeting her and about his and Jeremy's "arrangement."

Jeremy paused. "Uhm…no. Not yet. But I will," he added hastily.

"Okay. Well, don't worry," William reassured him. "I won't say anything." He felt relief flow through him.

He didn't have to admit his little deception to Brooke.

Yet.

***

William deliberately arrived early to meet Brooke, making it to the college theatre on time to catch the last few minutes of the children's play.

Signs all over the lobby announced *Welcome to the Haunted House* was playing today. Since it was the very end, no one was taking tickets any longer, and he quietly opened the door to the theatre and slipped inside.

He stood near the mezzanine, letting his eyes adjust to the dark. He focused on the stage, hearing the laughter of children in the audience. A funny, not-scary-looking witch stirred a cauldron, which appeared to have steam rising from it. Two ghosts stood nearby, along with what appeared to be a green alien and a skeleton. On one side, a pumpkin lit up, then faded into a plain orange, then lit up again. A moon glowed in the background.

Brooke had done an excellent job with the scenery and special effects. Judging from the sound of the kids' laughter and how they all seemed to stare raptly at the stage, he gathered the show was a hit.

The witch sang something about a spell, and the lights faded as her song finished. Moments later, they came on again, and now the alien and skeleton had turned into a girl and boy, and the ghosts had moved to the side.

The kids in the audience shrieked.

William grinned, feeling oddly proud of the work Brooke had done.

There were a few more lines, then the curtains closed. The applause was loud and enthusiastic and rang in his ears. The curtains opened again, and there were several curtain calls before the curtains closed again and the lights came on.

"That was excellent!" one mother near William declared as she led a group of children up the aisle.

"Yes, the best play they've done in the last three years," another agreed. "Wasn't it great how they had so many special effects?"

He'd have to tell Brooke about that comment.

He strolled over to the side, waiting for the majority of people to move up the aisle before he started down the opposite way.

He reached the stage, and went up the steps to the right. Parting the curtains on the side, he entered the controlled bedlam that was typical backstage, even after a performance.

Adults and children in a wide range of Halloween costumes from funny pirates to weird vampires were hugging each other, talking and laughing. Over and over, he heard, "Congratulations! Great show!" Some of the adults lugged scenery around, mostly fake trees and bushes. Two women dressed as witches passed, holding the cauldron, which no longer "steamed." A gypsy woman carried a small table and behind her, a teen held a broom and what looked like a model of a UFO.

"Do you know where I can find Brooke Perez?" William asked the gypsy.

She pointed. "Back there."

William followed her finger and saw Brooke on a ladder, spotted by a young woman, as she detached a fabric bat from a thin wire.

But he barely noticed her actions. Instead, he noticed how Brooke looked.

She wore a black skirt that wasn't particularly short—but it gave a good view of her shapely legs. Her turquoise sweater hugged her feminine curves. Finishing the outfit was a geometric black, silver and turquoise necklace with a matching bracelet and earrings. Her small feet were clad in simple black pumps.

It wasn't a very dramatic outfit, yet on Brooke, the effect was stunning.

William strode forward as she descended the stepladder.

His mind flashed back to two weeks ago, when she'd done the same thing, almost landing in his arms, their faces coming close together, their lips mere inches apart.

And he'd almost kissed her.

Brooke spotted him. "Hi, William! You're early."

As he reached the ladder, he noticed something else.

Around her slender left ankle, a silver bracelet glimmered. Suddenly, he was hit by an overwhelming urge to sweep Brooke into his arms and kiss her thoroughly. Something about that glinting bracelet on her slender ankle reminded him that Brooke was a beautiful, sensual woman.

"You look gorgeous." His voice was hoarse as he met her eyes.

She took the last step down. "Thanks."

"I mean it." He waved his hand, letting it sweep over her, taking in her whole presence. "You're the center of the stage."

She started to smile, and then her smile faded as he continued to stare at her.

He reached out, saw his own hand moving towards her as if in slow motion. He didn't recall stepping closer, but he must have, since he was able to cup her chin.

She tilted her head to gaze at him, and he brought his mouth close to hers. He hovered for just a second, inhaling her feminine cologne, hearing her breath hitch.

And then he brushed his lips against hers. And brushed them again. And lingered.

Her lips were soft and warm, and instinctively he pressed his own against hers.

She responded instantly, her hands moving to his shoulders, clutching him.

For a moment they stood, lips locked together, and he reveled in her kiss.

Someone coughed behind them. It was subtle, but loud enough to interrupt the electric moment.

Reluctantly, he broke the kiss as she loosened her hold on him.

The young woman he'd noticed before still stood near the ladder.

Will spared the student only a quick glance. Brooke encompassed his mind, his thoughts. He felt riveted by her presence and didn't want to look at anything else. For a long moment, they stared at each other.

Her cheeks flushed a beautiful rose color. Sounds

of chatter, the noises of furniture dragged nearby, all intruded on his mind a few seconds later.

Abruptly, Brooke stepped back, and looked towards her right.

"I'll take that." The jeans-clad young woman moved into Will's line of vision and gently took the fabric bat from Brooke.

"Oh, thanks, Adrielle." Brooke's voice was breathless. "William, this is Adrielle Morgan, the student director for scenery and design."

Will turned and shook the student's hand. He must have murmured something congenial because she smiled at him before heading backstage.

"Can I move that for you?" Will indicated the ladder.

"That would be a help." Brooke's cheek color was still bright, but she said nothing about their sudden kiss.

Will folded the ladder, and she led him backstage, pointing to an alcove with another ladder. "This is where we keep it."

Close up, he smelled her floral perfume again, a soft, feminine scent that enticed him.

"I did get a ride here with my co-worker," she said, and he noted her voice was still slightly breathless. "So we don't have to worry about my car."

"I'm ready whenever you are," Will told her.

"Let me just get my purse," she said and dashed backstage, where he assumed the dressing rooms were.

She was back out in a couple of minutes. As she walked towards him, holding her jacket and purse, the ankle bracelet glinted.

Something about that ankle bracelet made her look so sensual, so appealing. He was ready to kiss her again.

"Let's go!" she said brightly.

The late afternoon was cool, but typical for mid-October. Some clouds scooted across the blue sky, and a soft wind blew.

It took about forty-five minutes to get to the restaurant. Brooke spoke about the scenery for the show and some of the problems they'd had and how she'd solved them.

Will tried to pay attention, but he couldn't help wondering when he could kiss her again.

***

Wow, that was some kiss, Brooke thought for the hundredth time as they were shown to a table in the restaurant.

And here she'd been thinking William thought of her as a friend, like she thought of him. Well, that idea had flown out the window. You didn't kiss a friend the way he'd kissed her!

She'd wondered about him for days, trying to decide since he'd asked her out if he was viewing this more as a friends-only thing or a date-thing. She'd decided to dress up a little, apply more makeup than she'd worn with him previously, and to wear sexy shoes.

Remembering she had to help out at the theatre, she'd changed the sexy shoes to plain pumps, but still she'd tried to look pretty and feminine.

She guessed she had succeeded.

"Would you care for something from the bar? Or perhaps you'd like to see our wine list?" the waiter intoned.

They ordered red wine, and then studied the menu.

Brooke sneaked a peek at William. He wore a dark blue shirt with a blue and black striped tie, which brought out the blue in his eyes. He wore a black sports jacket and black pants, and while the outfit wasn't very dressy, it was more formal than anything she'd seen him wear in years.

She liked it.

He looked casually masculine, as if he hadn't put much thought into looking that way--as if he was born that way. Which he was, she thought, thinking back to the way he'd looked when they were younger. Maybe it was his broad shoulders, or the handsome yet masculine features on his face, or his engaging smile. Whatever it was, he was the kind of guy women noticed. And flirted with and chased after.

For tonight, she thought with a spurt of pleasure, he was *her* date.

Following on the heels of that was a disconcerting thought.

William was supposed to be her friend. *Her friend.* Not a boyfriend. Why was she having these romantic thoughts about him? Why did she feel this attraction? Well, maybe because he was a handsome man. But she wasn't going to think about him in that way. No.

She made a conscientious effort to keep their conversation light and friendly.

William ordered the cream of tomato soup and one of the evening's specials, steak with lobster tails. Brooke decided on the house salad and veal cordon bleu.

Once the waiter had taken their menus and

departed, she sipped her wine and helped herself to the homemade bread sitting in the basket on the table.

"Are things less hectic at the studio?" she asked, buttering the fragrant, warm bread.

William nodded. "It will be. Ben's coming back on Monday, so we'll return to our normal schedule."

They spoke about their jobs, and the conversation was congenial. She managed to keep things pleasant, but she forced herself not to sound overly effusive.

When William asked about her family, it seemed natural to say, "I'm going there tomorrow. Why don't you stop in? Then you can see everyone for yourself."

"I'd like that," he said with alacrity.

Brooke tried not to show the sudden consternation she felt. Why had she extended that invitation? What had she been thinking? William might be a friend, who knew her whole family, but she didn't have to invite him to see everyone in person. Although, maybe that would cement the idea their relationship was simply an "old friends" one.

She changed the subject and found herself telling him how a student had asked, last semester, in front of the entire class, if she was the daughter of Sharon Maloney-Perez, the famous soap opera star.

"Of course I said yes," Brooke said. "I tried to change the topic, but afterwards, several students came up to me and asked me about my mom, and did it give me 'pull' in show business, that kind of thing." She shook her head. "I told them how I wanted to be known for myself and my work and didn't talk about my mother. Someone said that was silly."

"How did you feel?" William asked, cutting his steak.

"Peculiar, like I had to defend myself for wanting to be independent. Then I felt—well, annoyed. I don't have to defend myself to anyone, not my students or others." She sighed. "It's so nice to be with a friend who knows my background, and I don't have to hide these things or answer questions." She smiled at him.

He gave her a look she couldn't analyze, long and unblinking.

The food was delicious, and Brooke enjoyed dinner, despite being a little on edge. She was relieved William kept the conversation light, as well.

After a sweet dessert of chocolate mousse, they left the restaurant. William put his hand lightly on her shoulder as they waited for the valet to bring his car. She asked him about his work for the following week, and he spoke about doing an interview with a well-known sculptor who lived in Sussex County. "We concentrate on Morris, but do some features on Sussex and Warren counties, especially on the arts or history," he said. "Like that Egyptian guy at your college."

She caught the faintest note of derision in his voice and had to keep from smiling. Was he jealous?

No, he shouldn't be, part of her mind argued.

They listened to music on the way back to her condo, a local station that played classic rock music. William didn't talk much, and she was fine sitting quietly, speaking briefly about his favorite football team, the Jets.

She made herself yawn when they reached her home, but invited him in for a glass of wine. He declined the wine, opting for a Coke, and she put on the TV, trying hard to create an atmosphere that wasn't too romantic.

When she returned from the kitchen with his soda, William sat on the couch, Tiger beside him. William stared at her, a strange expression on his face.

Brooke took a swig of her own soda. She didn't like feeling uncomfortable and almost never did around William. But right this minute, she felt strange.

She sat on the couch. Not too close to William, but not too far, either, or he'd think she was mad.

She wasn't. She was trying to keep things on an even keel, she told herself.

He sipped his soda silently.

"So what do you think of the newest Jets quarterback?" Brooke asked, forgetting the guy's name, but desperate to make pleasant conversation.

He went along with the topic. "He's very good and had a great record with his previous team, but of course, the whole team is still learning to work together as one unit."

Brooke nodded. "You're right. There's so much teamwork involved."

They spoke about the Jets for a few more minutes, then Brooke yawned again, this time for real.

Concern passed over his face. "You're tired. You must have had a long day, with the play and all."

She was automatically about to say no, she wasn't too tired, and then thought better of it. It had been hard trying to remain simply friendly with William, to forget that kiss, and maybe she was tired—and tense. She wouldn't mind going to sleep early.

"I am, a little," she agreed.

"I'll get going." William stood, looking disappointed. But what hit her again was how handsome and masculine he looked in his suit.

They walked to the door. "Thank you. This was such a lovely evening," she said. "The restaurant was great, and I had a wonderful time."

They reached the door.

Brooke looked up at William, and decided she'd give him a big hug.

But before she could move a muscle, he reached out. Placing one hand on her shoulder, he tilted her chin with his other hand and gazed directly into her eyes.

"Brooke." His voice was husky and so very male. A shiver crept along her spine.

His lips came down on hers, and the yearning that wound through Brooke was strong and unexpected, like a wave crashing on the sand. Without thought, she moved into his arms, and he held her tightly. He kissed her, hard, and all she could think was how good his kiss felt, how wonderful it felt to be held by him like this.

Then that little voice at the back of her mind poked her, reminding her William was supposed to be a friend. And she sure wasn't kissing him the way you kissed a mere friend.

She loosened her grip on William, and he stepped back.

They stared at each other for a moment, and Brooke had to force herself not to touch her lips, which felt blazingly hot after his kiss.

"Goodnight, Brooke," he said, his voice hoarse.

"Goodnight," she replied. Her voice was steady, but came out as more of a whisper.

He left, and she shut and locked the door, then leaned against it.

That was not a simple, friendly kiss. It was a whole lot more. And she liked it.

CHAPTER VII

Brooke didn't sleep well that night.

She tried reading the mystery, and though it was good, she had trouble concentrating on the book. She didn't want to read Derek's book, since she wanted to avoid thinking about men.

Once she switched off the light, she tossed and turned. Nate, Derek, and William bounced through her mind.

Especially William. What on earth was she doing kissing him? Especially an intense kiss like the one they'd shared?

She suspected he, too, had been surprised by the power of that kiss.

And Derek. She liked him, but she wasn't sure she wanted anything more than a casual relationship with him. Could she trust him?

She could trust William. But she wanted him to be her friend—period.

And Nate. She caught herself clenching her teeth. Nate had been completely untrustworthy. It was his fault she was having trouble sleeping right now.

She let out a frustrated groan and turned over.

She had to get some sleep. She forced herself to

think about Jeremy and how happy he'd been lately, and she finally fell asleep.

Sundays she usually slept in, but she woke up by nine o'clock and made herself coffee and oatmeal. She watched one episode of her mom's show, Tiger curled nearby, but grew restless. It was a few hours until she was going to her parents' house, and she chastised herself again for inviting William. What had she been thinking? Come to think of it, she hadn't even let her parents know—although, they'd never object to her having a friend join them for the afternoon and dinner. She quickly emailed them, afraid to call too early. Her mom almost always slept in on Sundays.

She had papers to finish grading, but felt too restless to work at home, so she drove to the college. The offices were deserted, and she was able to concentrate on the papers at hand and finish grading them in less than two hours.

She went from the theatre department's offices to the theatre, passing students walking throughout the campus. She checked on some of the props she and Adrielle had assembled. Satisfied, she glanced at her watch. It was almost one o'clock. No wonder her stomach rumbled.

She decided to grab lunch out and do some shopping on the way to her parents' house. She planned to stay a few hours, then check in on a rehearsal of the Tri County Players, a community group planning to perform Gilbert and Sullivan's operetta, *The Mikado*. Brooke had actually been in a production of the operetta once in a summer program, and she loved the music, so she'd been happy to help them. She'd attended a couple of rehearsals at the end of the summer and had finished the scenery plans, so at this point, all she had to do was make sure they could follow her instructions.

She went to the mall, ate a late lunch, and then spent time shopping for herself. She picked up a navy sweatshirt on sale—she could always use dark ones for backstage work—and then treated herself to a new pair of warm boots in a dark red color for fun.

She placed her purchases in her car's trunk, and her cellphone rang. Glancing at the display, she saw it was Janice, the director of the community show.

"Brooke?" Janice sounded disturbed.

"Hi, Janice." Brooke slammed her trunk down and got into her car, but didn't start the motor. Something was up. "How's everything?"

"Not good. Carissa quit."

Brooke thought rapidly. Carissa was a temperamental actress, who caused problems last year in a production, acting like a real prima donna. Brooke was surprised Janice had given her a role as one of the three little maids, but then, Carissa did have a lovely voice. And Pitty Sing did a lot of singing in the show, almost as much as Yum Yum, the lead of the three little maids.

"Yesterday we got into an argument, over her costume. She didn't think it was as nice as the other two maids' costumes. I just got a call from her, and she said she quit."

"Oh dear," Brooke said sympathetically. The show was due to open in three weeks. It was going to be hard for them to find a replacement and train her by then.

"I can't replace her. I'm one of the maids myself."

"What about the understudy?"

"She's studying all three maids' parts. And her voice is pleasant, but not great. So we have to keep her as an understudy," Janice said, her voice grim. "Hal and I talked all last night and this morning about this."

Hal was the president of the theatre group and had a leading role in the production as a noble gentleman.

In an instant, Brooke knew what she was going to ask.

"Please, Brooke, would you consider playing the part?" she asked.

Brooke's first thought was yes, then no. Then yes again.

She had always loved *The Mikado*. And she knew the play well, probably even remembered a lot of the music. She'd heard them rehearsing during her last two visits to the community theatre, found her CD of the music, and listened to it in the car last week.

But, it had been at least three years since she had performed onstage and that had been a small role, with no singing. It would be a lot of work to get up to speed on this show.

Then again, she did have the time. She was caught up with her classwork, exams wouldn't be until December, the main production at the college was moving along smoothly, and the children's play was over.

"Please? We'll do whatever it takes," Janice cajoled.

She started to say yes, then forced herself to say, "I'll think about it. I'll be there tonight so we can talk." It would be better, she knew, to think this over carefully before making that commitment.

"Oh, it would be so wonderful if you would!" Janice said. She rushed on before Brooke could say anything else. "This would be perfect for us, for the theatre. You'd be saving our production. And Hal and I know you would do a fine job."

"Well, it won't be easy, and I'm not sure I'd do a great job," Brooke said slowly.

"Yes, you will, I'm sure of it."

"I'll think about it," Brooke reiterated.

As she drove to her parents' house, Brooke was sure of one thing.

Acting in this production would keep her pretty busy and keep her mind off other things. Like men.

***

Of course, her family had opinions on her being in the musical.

Her mother, Jeremy, and Rebecca thought Brooke should participate.

"You know you'd have a good time, even though it's work," Rebecca said.

"And you're already doing their scenery," her mom pointed out. "You're there a lot the last few weeks before the opening anyway."

Troy and his wife, Rebecca's husband, and Brooke's dad said she should only do it if she was certain she had the time.

"It's a big commitment," her dad stated.

William, when he arrived, joined in the discussion. "If you would enjoy doing it, and it wouldn't give you stress, you should do it. But if it would be a hassle, don't."

Brooke listened and weighed everyone's opinions. She was able to maneuver things so she and William were constantly with members of her family and not alone. He didn't protest, although a couple of times she caught him staring at her. Once, Rebecca whispered that she'd call Brooke to catch up, and another time Jeremy sent her a quizzical look. Otherwise, everyone acted as if William was merely an old friend stopping in to visit for a few hours.

Which he was, Brooke reminded herself. And yet, when he joined them, she felt more energized, more alive.

She glanced at her parents. They'd had a whirlwind romance. Would she ever have that experience?

They ate dinner early, since everyone had to scatter. It was lasagna, garlic bread and salad her parents had brought in from a gourmet marketplace. Jeremy whispered it wasn't as good as Nicole's, but their mother rarely cooked anything besides simple dishes, and their housekeepers hadn't been gourmet cooks, either. The food was good, if not spectacular, and she was hungry. Troy's little girl kept them laughing during most of the meal, and they managed to discuss politics and the upcoming election without much controversy.

Rebecca was tired from her pregnancy, and she and her husband left right after dinner. Brooke was glad of the excuse to leave early, too. She wanted to speak to Janice and Hal and check on the production. And she wanted to leave before she really had time alone with William.

"I'm leaving now, too," William announced. "I'll walk you out."

97

After the goodbyes, they walked out to the driveway. Brooke remained silent, wondering if William had something on his mind.

"I'll call you this week," he said. "Hopefully, we can get together again soon."

"Let me see what's going on with *The Mikado* first."

He nodded, his eyes on her face. Clouds blew in the darkening sky.

The drive back took a little over an hour, since Brooke had to go past her condo and into the next town. She felt a little bad she hadn't spent much time at all with Tiger today, but cats didn't need as much human interaction as dogs, she reminded herself.

She concentrated on thinking about the production, pushing William—and Derek—to the back of her mind. Nate—she didn't even want to *think* his name. She made a face and banished him to the back recesses of her brain.

She reviewed the pros and cons of doing the show in her mind. First, it was already familiar, meaning she wouldn't have to go crazy learning her lines or the songs. Second, she did enjoy being on the stage, though not as much as setting the stage. Still, it could be fun as well as work. And she hadn't performed in several years, so it might be a good thing for her. Not for her resume, necessarily, but to test herself, make sure she still had it in her—whatever "it" was. While she didn't have the burning desire to be on stage the way her mother always had, she did enjoy the occasional performance on her mom's soap opera.

She and her siblings, and a couple of times their dad, occasionally had performed with their mother in

All My Relatives. The Perez kids played nieces and nephews of her mother's character who lived on the west coast and showed up for sporadic visits. When they performed, they donated their pay to charity, so it was fun to do every few years.

And it kept them on their toes. You never knew when the experience might help with a speech or some kind of public performance.

So here was a chance to be on stage again, to brush up her skills. It might be fun.

She was up to date on her work for the college, and she did enjoy having a variety of work to do.

Plus, they needed her. The group was in a real bind.

The only negative was it would take a big chunk of her free time in the next few weeks. But since she had performed before, and had performed *this* role before, she didn't think she'd feel too stressed about it.

Once she arrived at the country club where the community group rehearsed—they'd do the actual show at the local high school—Janice and Hal practically pounced on her.

"You'll do it, won't you?" Hal asked anxiously.

"Please? We wouldn't ask if we didn't think you could do a great job," Janice added.

Brooke smiled. "Okay, you talked me into it."

Janice squealed and gave Brooke an enormous hug. Hal stepped in to hug her as soon as Janice let go.

"What a relief," Janice said. "Now, Brooke, I think the first thing to do is give you another copy of the script…"

She chattered and made suggestions for rehearsals if Brooke wanted extra practice. When the other actors arrived, it wasn't long until everyone knew Brooke would participate in the show.

"This will be great for us," a woman named Beverly remarked.

Hal clapped his hands. "Okay, let's get to work everyone!"

Several hours flew by. Brooke read from the script, some of the lines coming back to her in surprisingly whole pieces. By ten o'clock, Hal announced they should conclude for the night, and he'd see everyone on Tuesday.

Brooke drove home and found Tiger waiting. She hurried into the kitchen, but found he still had food in his dish. She added more, gave him fresh water, and then sat on the couch. He jumped up beside her, and she petted him.

"Sorry, I won't be around much the next few weeks," she said. He blinked. She wondered if he'd be lonely.

As if to say it wasn't a big deal, he jumped off the couch and went to get a drink of water.

It had been a long day, and she had been up early. Brooke yawned. She'd thought about tossing some laundry into her washer, but decided to get ready for bed instead. It would be a busy week.

She was tired enough she didn't think too much about William, or Derek, before she drifted off.

***

Brooke entered her office at the college on Tuesday afternoon and dropped her tote bag and purse on her desk.

"Hello!" Bert's cheerful voice startled her, and he popped up from behind his desk, like a jack-in-the-box.

"I didn't mean to scare you," he said, observing her expression. "I'm crawling around back here, trying to untangle some wires so I can plug in my laptop."

"It's okay," she said, waving her hand. She sat and opened her tote to go over plans for her classes the next couple of days, and maybe, take another look at the script she'd studied last night.

"Hey, I hear you're going to be in the Tri County Players' production of *The Mikado*. Good for you. I'll have to come watch a performance. I've never seen you act."

"Wow. News travels fast," Brooke said. She was flattered the head of her department might want to see her. She hoped he wouldn't be overly critical. "It's been a few years since I actually performed on stage."

"You'll be fine. You're a natural, and I'm sure you didn't forget the acting lessons you've had."

"How did you know?" she asked.

He grinned. "It's all over the place. I saw it on Facebook. I'm acquainted with Hal. It's on their website, they're sending out notices on Facebook and Twitter. I even heard a spot on the radio about the show, featuring the 'well-known TV actress, Brooke Perez.'"

She rolled her eyes. "Well-known TV actress? That's an exaggeration."

"Well, you have been on TV," Bert said, "on your mother's soap opera."

"Appearing once every couple of years hardly makes me well-known," Brooke pointed out, but she smiled. Really, it was kind of nice the theatre group was so excited about having her. "I hope I live up to everyone's expectations."

"You will," he affirmed.

They were interrupted by music from her cellphone. "Walk Like an Egyptian."

"I'll call back later." She pulled a folder from her tote, sat, and got to work.

Bert didn't say another word until he left an hour later and said goodbye.

At that point, Brooke listened to Derek's message. He was thinking about her. Calling him back, she got his voice mail.

She went home, changed to jeans and a casual top, and sat with Tiger. She petted him, his fur soft and warm beneath her fingers

"Don't you worry. I'll find a good place for you," Brooke vowed.

Maybe she should ask at the theatre. A lot of the actors there loved animals.

She got up, checked her email, then realized she only had a few minutes before her dinner with her brother, followed by rehearsal at the theatre.

She met Jeremy with seconds to spare. They discussed the play, then switched the topic to him and Nicole. She was surprised to learn Jeremy still hadn't told Nicole about their famous family. Previously, she'd been gentle in her suggestions he should tell Nicole before she found out about the Perezes herself. On Sunday, she'd told him outright he had to tell her. But when she discovered he still hadn't mentioned it, she became more emphatic.

"You really need to tell her. If she finds out some other way, she'll be mad you didn't tell her the truth."

"Do you really think so? I just want to be liked for myself, not for our famous family."

"I know. But you've been going out for a while, and it's obvious she likes you for yourself," Brooke said. "Trust me, if a guy didn't tell me something like this, *I'd* be upset."

Jeremy stared at her, then sighed. "I guess I should."

Once at the theatre, Brooke forgot about their conversation and concentrated on acting her part. She found she enjoyed it, but there was a certain nervousness she felt simmering underneath. People were expecting a lot from her. What if she didn't measure up?

She didn't check her cellphone until she got home that evening. She saw she'd missed another call from Derek and one from William, too.

It was ten o'clock. She could call them back, but at this point she was tired. She decided to get ready for bed, watch a little TV, and go to bed early.

She'd speak to them both tomorrow.

***

Wednesday, Brooke only taught one class, but she had work to do with the stage productions going on at Quemby—both with the theatre and non-theatre majors—and hoped to sneak in a little more time to practice a couple of the songs for the show. She was planning to rehearse with her friend, Kelly, next week. She called both Derek and William and got voice mails again. Shrugging mentally, she applied herself to her work, then went home early to practice in private.

The rehearsal that evening went fairly well, and

she felt confident when she returned to her condo. She found both Derek and William had called again while her cellphone was off, and once she'd showered and plopped down on the couch with Tiger, she lit a vanilla-scented candle and called them both back, starting with Derek.

He picked up at once and told her he was back in New Jersey.

"How about we get together this weekend?" he asked.

Brooke thought it might be a good thing to spend the weekend concentrating on the play, which was due to open the first weekend of November, only two and a half weeks from today. She felt so confused about William, and Derek—men in general, really. A break in her routine might be a very good thing for her.

She explained about the performance and how she'd have almost no free time until after the show closed. "And the week after is the theatre majors' student-run show at Quemby. And the week after that is the non-theatre majors' production, although I have little to do with that, actually. So, how about if we get together after *The Mikado* is over?"

There was silence for a moment. "Are you giving me the brush-off?" Derek asked, his voice cool.

"No, just a postponement. You were away," she reminded him, "and now I have a big commitment." Annoyance crept into her tone. It was okay for him to be busy with work, but not her?

"You're right. We've both had work-related commitments. By the way, I was reading up on you some more," he added with a chuckle. "Your family is even more famous than I realized a few weeks ago."

The annoyance had diminished when he'd said she was right, but now it came back. "You could say they are." She didn't try to keep the prickly note out of her voice. *Don't tell me I'm going to have to deal with the same stuff Jeremy's had to deal with.*

"We have a lot in common," he went on, as if he didn't notice her tone.

Really? Maybe she was tired and overly sensitive.

"How about I call you in a few days when I have more time to talk?" she asked, deliberately mellowing her voice.

"That would be good. Let's talk on Friday, okay?"

She agreed, said goodbye, and clicked off.

"*Men*," she said to Tiger.

He stared at her.

"Present company excepted," she added.

Next, she called William.

"Hey, Brooke!" he said cheerfully. "How're rehearsals going?"

She told him about the practices, how she was continuing to oversee the scenery and props, and the fun, and pressures, of being back onstage.

"I love the show, so that was one incentive to be in it," she confided. "And it's not bad being in front of an audience every once in a while in my business. But my real love is the staging and scenery, setting the scene for these productions."

"And you're great at it," William said. "Is it hard to do both simultaneously?"

"A little," she admitted. She relaxed into the couch, breathing the soft vanilla scent of the candle. "I may be distracted by one when I'm doing the other.

105

For this production, though, once I'm on stage, I'll have to concentrate on that. I got lucky. A couple of my students from the college volunteered to help with the scenery when they heard I was going to act in the show." She'd been grateful when Adrielle and Geraldo had offered to help.

William asked about seeing her this weekend, and she told him she was busy with rehearsals and she'd have to get together with him after the show.

He didn't ask her if it was a brush-off.

They spoke for a few more minutes, then Brooke got off the phone, checked her email, and went to sleep.

At least, she thought as she pulled the covers up, William had asked about the show and her reactions to it. Unlike Derek, who she still thought might be a little too wrapped up in himself.

She sighed and closed her eyes. She could hear, in her mind, the strains of "Three Little Maids" playing in the background.

***

William plugged in his cellphone to recharge overnight and sighed.

Speaking to Brooke was always nice, but seeing her in person was so much better.

And it looked like it might be a few weeks until he actually saw her in person.

He gritted his teeth. Was it true she was busy with rehearsals? Or was she busy with that Derek character? Or even someone else?

Or maybe she just didn't want to be busy with *him*?

He sighed. He didn't usually think so negatively. But he knew his feelings for Brooke were deepening, and he hoped she felt something for him, too.

He didn't have to go into work until later tomorrow, and he was too restless to sleep right away. He'd heard Ryan turn in earlier, and a glance at the clock showed him it was a little after eleven.

He went into the living room, grabbed the remote, and channel surfed for a while. He finally settled in to watch a crime investigation show he liked.

But Brooke remained firmly on his mind.

He'd overheard her say something on Sunday to Jeremy about telling Nicole about their famous family. He wondered again about saying something to Brooke regarding how he'd had Jeremy arrange for him to "run into" her at Nicole and Marla's home.

He should say something when he saw her again, he thought, guilt rushing through him.

And...he didn't want to wait two and a half weeks to see her.

CHAPTER VIII

Saturday, they had a complete rehearsal. Brooke was relieved, since rehearsing one act at a time had been good in the beginning, but now they were getting near the finish line. The show would open in less than two weeks, on a Thursday evening, and she needed to get the feel of the entire production.

The rehearsal went fairly well. She only flubbed one line, and her singing was good. One of the leading men forgot his words during the second act, so she wasn't the only one. She felt relieved when she got home. She'd risen early, and on her way home from the rehearsal, she picked up a few groceries. Now that it was nearly six o'clock, all she had to do was relax for the rest of the evening.

She popped a frozen pizza into the oven, threw in a load of wash, and checked her email. She hadn't seen Tiger when she first came in, but now he suddenly appeared, and she discovered he liked pizza—both the cheese and the sauce.

After dinner and a quick shower, Brooke sat on her couch, wondering what to do with this empty Saturday night. Normally she went out, if not on a date, then with friends. Occasionally, if neither she nor

Jeremy had plans, they might take in a movie together. But she guessed he'd be busy with Nicole.

Rebecca had said several times that she and her husband liked to take a Saturday evening, at least once a month, to do nothing. Maybe they'd watch a DVD or play Scrabble, or sometimes just read and do their own thing. "Everyone needs some quiet time," her older sister would declare.

But Brooke didn't need as much quiet time as her sister—both because of Rebecca's quieter personality and because, as a physician, she often put in long hours, longer than Brooke's. Brooke stretched and looked at the TV. She didn't feel like quiet time right now.

She decided to watch two episodes of her mom's show, but didn't want to watch more than that. She was almost caught up anyway. Afterwards, she read. She didn't want to pick up Derek's book right now. She wanted to *not* think about men. So, she settled in to finish the mystery.

She read quickly, and by ten-thirty, she'd reached the end.

Sitting back, she glanced around.

Sometime during the second episode of her mother's soap opera, Tiger had scampered off the couch to investigate who knows what. Without him, she felt very alone.

Automatically, she reached for her cellphone. Without another thought, she found William's cell number and pushed the call button. What was she doing?

Before she could disconnect, he picked up. "Hello? Brooke?" He must have recognized her number.

"Oh, I—sorry, I hope I didn't wake you." Or interrupt something, she thought. What if he was out with another woman?

Well, maybe she'd want to know that.

"Not at all. Just sitting here watching 'Back to the Future' for the hundredth time," he replied.

"Oh, I love that movie," she said, leaning back into the couch.

"Me, too. How's the play going?"

She told him about her long rehearsal today, and then added how tired she was, so he wouldn't think she was lying when she said she'd have no time to see him this weekend. As she said the words, she realized she *was* tired. She yawned.

"It's a lot of work," William said. "I admire you for doing this play."

"Thanks." She asked him about his job, but was careful not to inquire about what he'd been doing this weekend.

He told her about a few of the features he'd videoed and edited. When Brooke suppressed another yawn, he said, "I can hear you're tired. I'll give you a call in a few days."

She said goodbye and disconnected, staring at the phone.

She wanted to be simply friends with William. So why was she calling him on a Saturday night?

***

Sunday, Brooke had plans to meet Janice and the other "maid" from the show, a woman named Louise, so they could practice their songs for an hour or so. An

110

unexpected call from Jeremy had her meeting him for lunch first.

Jeremy was despondent. A friend had shown Nicole an article in the hated "National Snoop" magazine, which revealed he came from a famous family. Worse, the article claimed he was using Nicole's TV show to get into show business, and Nicole had apparently felt hurt and betrayed.

"I blew it, Brooke," he said.

"I can understand how frustrated you feel," Brooke said, weighing her words. She'd never seen Jeremy look so upset. "But think about how she feels."

"She's mad."

"And hurt, I imagine," Brooke pointed out. "I would be. Here she is, falling head over heels for you…"

Jeremy stared at her. "Do you think so?"

"I can see it in her face," Brooke told him. "And then she finds out you're not really who she thought you were."

"It's not like I'm a criminal or anything," Jeremy protested.

"All you did was deceive her by hiding your real identity," Brooke said. "I'd be hurt and angry if it happened to me. Tell me, Jer, how would you feel if you found out Nicole came from a famous family?"

"I wouldn't care," he said quickly.

Brooke pointed out how hurt Jeremy had been when his old girlfriend, Monica, had used him to get close to his family for the purpose of furthering her acting aspirations. As she observed her brother, Brooke was sure he was even more upset now. He truly cared about Nicole.

They paused to give their orders to the waiter, and then Brooke spoke again. "You were devastated someone would use you like that, and I don't blame you. Nicole must feel the same way, devastated."

"I didn't use her."

"But you hid the truth." She reached over and gave his hand a squeeze. "She feels used, too—like you thought she wasn't important enough for you to tell her the truth."

"But I've always treated her well."

"I know! You're a wonderful person and a great boyfriend, except, now, she's hurt. If you had told her first, I think she would have had a different reaction. Maybe she would have been annoyed, but it wouldn't have been like this."

He considered her words, then nodded.

"So, the question is..." Brooke took a deep breath."What do you want to do?"

"Do?" He stared at her.

"Do you want to just let her walk away, or do you want to try to mend the tear in your relationship? Do you want to fight for her?"

Jeremy's face was pale. "I don't want to lose her," he said. After a moment, he repeated the words. "I don't want to lose her."

Brooke sat back. "So, what do you think you should do?" she asked him quietly. She hoped he'd try to make up with Nicole. Nicole was nice and clearly adored him. Brooke liked her and thought they were good together.

"I've got to apologize," Jeremy said, "and I've got to make her see that we belong together."

"I think you do," Brooke agreed.

In the meantime, a little sisterly help might be in order.

Maybe she should also speak to Nicole.

***

Monday afternoon, Brooke finished up some work at the college, then drove to Jeremy's. He had told her he had to work until dinner time, but she needed to see Nicole before he came home.

She hoped he wouldn't be annoyed, but she wanted to put in a good word for him. He was such a wonderful person, and Nicole *had* to see that. She had to.

She had a key to Jeremy's home and waited there, grading papers, for almost an hour until she spotted Nicole's car pulling into her driveway across the street. She put aside her things, waiting five minutes for Nicole to get settled, then left the house and locked the door. After placing her tote in her car, she approached Nicole's home.

She rang the doorbell, and Nicole opened it.

She looked genuinely surprised to see Brooke. Her face was wan, and her usually lively expression was missing.

"May I come in?" Brooke asked.

"Ugh—okay," Nicole said, stepping aside. "Want some soda or coffee?"

Brooke accepted coffee and followed Nicole into the kitchen. After Nicole started the coffee, she sat opposite Brooke at the kitchen table.

"I know you're angry with my brother," Brooke said. "He doesn't know I'm here, but I wanted to speak to you. I understand why you feel like you do. I really do. But I wanted to tell you a little about why he hid our family history from you."

"I should have known." Nicole ran a hand through her hair. "The signs were there that Jeremy came from a rich or famous family. I didn't want to see them. And I should have. After what I went through with my old boyfriend...well, you don't want to hear about that."

Brooke felt sympathy for Nicole. It sounded like she'd had her own rough experiences. "But I do," she declared. "Don't blame yourself. I'm actually annoyed at Jeremy for keeping it a secret for so long. I warned him you might find out, and he should come clean before that happened. But did he listen? Men," she added, a note of disgust in her voice.

Nicole smiled at Brooke's tone. "Yeah, men," she repeated. "He did tell me some girl used him to get to your mom."

"Yes, she had a warped idea that by getting close to Jeremy, and all of us, she could further her acting career." Brooke frowned.

Nicole got up to pour the coffee for Brooke, adding milk, and then sat with her soda.

The aroma of coffee was rich, and Brooke breathed it in. "Jeremy was devastated when he found out," Brooke said. She blew on the hot liquid, then took a sip. It was good. "I never saw him so upset—'til yesterday. Monica really hurt him. After that, he was very suspicious of women, and never told *anyone* about our background. Over and over, he said he wanted someone who cared about him for himself."

"But I do!" Nicole cried. "I lo-liked him for who he was. Is. I never wanted him to be anyone but himself."

"I think he was slowly coming to realize that," Brooke said. "And I think he was going to tell you. We'd discussed it recently. I just wished he'd done it a day or two earlier."

Nicole sighed. "I wish he'd told me, too. But he hid it. And yes, I know he had a reason, but he didn't trust me." There were tears in her eyes. "Maybe a part of him was out to have a good time. Maybe he didn't care if I found out eventually because then he'd be on to the next girlfriend."

"No, Nicole. I never saw him act the way he does around you—never, not even with Monica. He adores you. That's why he put off telling you, because you mean so much to him, and he didn't want to jeopardize your relationship."

Nicole stared at Brooke. "That's hard to believe," she said, her voice low.

"Believe it." Brooke leaned forward, grasping Nicole's hand. "Nicole, I hope you think of me as a friend, as well as Jeremy's sister. I promise you, he cares. I've never ever seen him act the way he does with you. And I've never seen him so despondent as…well, since this weekend, when you had your, uh, disagreement." Tears sprang to her own eyes as she spoke. "Please, please give him another chance. I know he's been calling, and I know you're upset, but you two are so wonderful together."

Nicole shook her head. "It's my…experience…rich guys don't want lasting relationships with average girls like me. They want to have fun with us, yes, but that's it. Then they go back to their socialite girlfriends when it's time to get serious."

"No," Brooke exclaimed. "Jeremy's not like that at all!"

"My last boyfriend was." Nicole's voice had turned bitter. "What reason do I have to believe Jeremy's going to be any different?"

"Because he is," Brooke insisted. "I promise you. Please, give him another chance."

"I don't know if he wants another chance," Nicole said, withdrawing her hand. "And I don't know if I can give him that and trust him, even if that *is* what he wants."

"Promise me you'll think about it," Brooke urged. "Please?"

Nicole hesitated.

"My brother is one of the best people I know. All I'm asking is that you be open-minded and give him a chance, okay?"

Nicole stared at Brooke. Brooke held her breath, hoping Nicole would realize how special her brother was, how much he did care for her.

Nicole drew a shaky breath. "I'll think about it."

Brooke smiled. "Thank you." She got up and hugged Nicole.

Nicole hugged her back, clinging a little.

Brooke decided to leave while Nicole seemed willing to consider giving Jeremy a chance, not wishing to overstay her welcome. She finished her coffee, got up to leave, and hugged Nicole again. "Thank you."

"Thank you," Nicole said.

Brooke hurried back to her car, got in and drove away. She was glad Jeremy didn't know she'd visited Nicole. She'd tell him later, of course, but hoped Nicole would actually speak to him first.

***

The ringing of the phone later that night startled Brooke as she reviewed one of the songs for the show.

It was Jeremy. He wanted to make up with Nicole and thought if he cooked her one of the dinners she'd demonstrated, it might do the trick.

Brooke smiled, then took a deep breath. "Go for it," she urged him. "I think she'll be delighted." She didn't want to say anything yet about speaking to Nicole.

"Do you think so?" he asked anxiously.

"Yes," she replied. "I really do." She sure hoped so.

"Okay, then I won't meet you for dinner on Tuesday," he finished.

Brooke almost laughed when Nicole called less than a half hour later.

Nicole wanted to make up with Jeremy. She admitted Brooke's talk—and a call from her old boyfriend—had made her see the light, and she wanted to give Jeremy another chance.

"I want to make him dinner," she said. ""I know you usually meet him on Tuesdays for dinner."

"I think making him dinner is a great idea," Brooke said, forcing herself not to chuckle. She went on to tell Nicole if she "cancelled" her Tuesday dinner with Jeremy, he might get suspicious.

She didn't want to give away the fact Jeremy was already making dinner for Nicole.

Nicole agreed to plan dinner for Wednesday, and when they said goodbye, Brooke jumped up, spun around the room and clapped her hands.

"This is great!" she declared. They both wanted to make up! And, oddly, in the same way.

Tiger looked at her quizzically.

"Isn't this funny?" she asked him, then leaned down to stroke him. When she straightened, she took off for the kitchen to get him a treat and pour herself a glass of wine.

Yippee!

Later, she wondered if her own romantic entanglements would ever get solved.

***

Nicole and Jeremy did make up, and by Saturday, Nicole and Marla had a Halloween party planned. Brooke was glad to go. She'd had a complete rehearsal that afternoon, which went fairly smoothly with only a few missed cues, so she got there a little late.

William had left her a message that he was working 'til eight and so he'd be late and not in costume. Since it was an impromptu party, half the guests had no costumes, while the other half did.

Brooke had dug up an old cowgirl costume she'd worn a few years ago, and she felt light-hearted and happy when she reached Nicole's home.

The party was fun. It was so wonderful to see her brother and Nicole looking joyous, their arms around each other. When William arrived, she spent some time with him, but with the group of about twenty people who were there, they were constantly with others.

He asked her about the play, and she answered general questions.

"I'm working next Friday night, but I'll be there Saturday night for the performance," he told her.

She was surprised. "Oh, you don't have to come." She knew Jeremy and Nicole were planning to attend, but really didn't expect anyone else she knew except for Adrielle and the others who were helping out. Really, she didn't have that big a role.

"I want to," he said simply.

She couldn't help the spurt of pleasure that rushed through her.

"And, Brooke," he began, "there's something I've been meaning to—"

Nicole appeared. "Brooke, can I speak to you?" She looked excited.

Brooke sent William an apologetic look. "I'll be back later." She followed Nicole into the kitchen, where they were alone.

"I'd really like," Nicole said, her face suddenly serious, "if you'd be one of my bridesmaids."

"Oh! I'd love to!" Brooke exclaimed, and throwing her arms around Nicole, hugged her future sister-in-law.

They discussed the wedding and Nicole's other attendants for a few minutes.

When she returned to where William stood a few minutes later, he was talking to Scott about his father's heart problem, and she didn't want to interrupt.

Tired from the long rehearsal, she left the party before midnight, and seeing her getting ready to leave, William said his goodbyes too and walked her out. Two other couples left with them.

"I'll see you next weekend," William said, and bending forward, gave Brooke a quick, friendly kiss.

119

CHAPTER IX

Brooke moved about the controlled chaos backstage on Saturday evening, doing a final check on the scenery. Adrielle walked with her, checking the fake trees and lanterns, while voices from the audience grew louder as more people entered the auditorium. Some kind of horn blared briefly, and Brooke heard the plucked strings of a few violins, followed by the rumble of a drum as the musicians warmed up.

This was her last chance to check the scenery before Adrielle took over. She trusted Adrielle, but still, it was her usual job, and she wanted to do a final check. Once the show began, she would have no time to do anything with the scenery.

Geraldo adjusted a light and gave her a thumbs-up before returning to work.

Janice spoke to her assistant, and they nodded as she passed.

"Curtain in ten minutes," he said.

"I'm ready." And she was. The familiar fluttering filled her stomach—only a fluttering, thank goodness. Since she'd been on stage since she was a child she'd never been troubled by true stage fright, just a twinge of uncertainty. It comforted her to know it was still there, like a familiar friend. Just enough to keep her sharp.

"Let's peek out," she said to Adrielle.

From stage left, she moved the curtain and peered into the auditorium, which was filling rapidly. Voices were raised in conversation, and someone burst into laughter. Someone else called, "Over here, Hank!" and a man waved to another man in the aisle.

She could see the audience quite clearly, although once the lights dimmed, she knew she'd barely see the first few rows. Near the center, a few rows back, she caught sight of Jeremy and Nicole, Marla and Scott—and were those her parents?

She sighed. They didn't have to come—she'd told them it was no big deal—but in their usual fashion, they were there to support her.

"My parents are out there," she told Adrielle.

Adrielle grinned. "I'm not surprised."

Brooke peeked out one more time. She saw William moving down the aisle, towards an empty seat in Jeremy's row. She thought she saw Connie and Ernie not far behind him. Wow! And was that—holy cow—a few rows back, was that Derek?

She stepped back quickly. William here and so was Derek? Now, she did have butterflies for real.

"Five minutes," a woman named Jodi said as she moved through the crowd backstage.

A clarinet played a scale, and she smelled heavy stage makeup as one of the women in the chorus hurried past her.

"Good luck," Adrielle said and melted into the shadows on the side.

"Places, places," Jodi called as she moved among the actors.

Brooke scampered to look one more time in the

mirror. Wearing a black wig and the Japanese outfit, she almost didn't recognize herself. She grabbed her fan and went to join the other three maids at the side of the stage, arriving as the auditorium lights dimmed.

She was not one of the first on stage, but she watched the men in the opening number move swiftly and silently to their places.

Suddenly, it was all business. There was no William, or Derek, or family. No one she had to impress. She was simply "Pitti-Sing."

The curtain rose, and the comedy unfolded. The wonderful music filled her ears, and she immersed herself in the story. Before she knew it, she and the other two "maids" joined the townspeople on stage, giggling, and launched into their signature song, "Three Little Maids."

"Three little maids from school are we…" they sang together.

The number ended to thunderous applause. They waited until it had died down to continue speaking. She looked at the audience without really seeing them, staying in character, speaking the lines she knew. She was no longer an actor on the stage. She was a "little maid," one of three sisters.

Somewhere, in the back of her brain, she knew their song went well. A glance at the audience once or twice gave her a blur of faces, no one specific. But some smiles were apparent.

Before she knew it, the act ended, and the curtain came down to loud applause. She could distinctly hear her father's, "Yay Brooke!" over other exclamations and had to smile. He was a sweetie.

Dorothy, the secretary for the theatre group who

had a part in the chorus, murmured from behind her, "Did you see that? Janice is right. Every seat is taken and there are people standing in the back."

"Standing room only?" another woman repeated. "Wow. I knew this was being promoted heavily, but didn't expect that."

"Gilbert and Sullivan has always been popular," a woman named May said.

"Not just that. It's because Brooke is performing. A lot of people want to see her," Janice said.

Brooke turned and stared at Janice. "Really?"

"Of course. You're famous, my dear, and people want to see you!" She beamed.

"Do you think so?" Brooke wasn't so naïve that she'd think her name wouldn't help the play, but would it really make that much difference?

"Plus, all these people kept calling the box office, reserving tickets, and saying they were your friends," Janice added.

Brooke hurried back to the ladies' dressing area, to check her makeup. They assembled for the second act and once again, Brooke immersed herself in her part.

Playing the sister of the lead young woman, Yum-Yum, was a blast, and she felt fully in character, saying her lines, singing with the others, truly being part of the ensemble. Before she knew it, they had reached the conclusion and sang the rousing finish, the whole cast assembled on stage. Their voices rose as they harmonized and sang about their good fortune and joy.

The curtain closed, and the audience went crazy, clapping, cheering, and whistling.

The curtain parted, and the entire cast moved forward.

Brooke could swear she heard Jeremy's and Nicole's shouts above the din of the crowd.

The players took center stage with some of the supporting cast. When it was Brooke's turn to go out, the applause surprised her. The noise was thunderous.

She could see the first few rows more clearly now. William stood, shouting, "Bravo" for all to hear. Her parents stood, Jeremy and Nicole stood, Marla and Scott—Derek even—Rebecca and her husband...

She moved back so the next main characters could take their bows, and the applause was wonderful for them, too.

Finally, after the lead actors had each received their own applause, the entire cast linked hands again and moved forward, then pointed to the conductor and orchestra.

The whole audience stood, clapping and cheering.

When the final curtain came down, the actors congratulated each other, hugging and giving high-fives.

"Wonderful performance!" Janice declared.

"We were all great!" exclaimed John, who played the Mikado.

"They loved us!" Shane, who played Nanki-Poo, the male lead, said.

"Our best performance yet!"

"Lots of people are waiting outside to congratulate you all," Adrielle announced.

Her parents were probably among them. Knowing they'd want to take a photo, Brooke followed Janice and a few other actors out the side door into a hallway filled with people.

"Brooke, over here." She caught sight of William, waving wildly.

He stood there with—wow—a bouquet filled with autumn flowers.

Next to him was her family, Connie and Ernie and—Derek! With a bunch of roses!

Uh-oh.

Brooke felt an urge to groan, but it passed, and she kept the smile on her face. It had been a great performance, and she'd concentrate on that.

She'd have to treat both William and Derek as good friends.

Which was what they were, right?

She moved forward and was engulfed in a huge hug by first her father, then mother.

"We're so proud of you," her mom gushed. "What an outstanding performance, Brooke. And really, the whole ensemble was wonderful."

Surrounded by all her friends and family, it was easy to speak to everyone, give hugs and simple kisses to William and Derek both. Then, she had to spend ten minutes posing for photos with every friend and family member. By the time they finished, she couldn't wait to remove the heavy theatrical makeup and get into normal clothes.

"Why don't we all have a snack?" Nicole suggested, eyeing the group.

"Great idea!" Brooke agreed. At least in a public venue, she could be friendly with everyone and not spend time alone with either William or Derek.

"We already have cake and ice cream at my place," Nicole said.

They decided that would be perfect. Everyone went on ahead, and Brooke returned to the dressing room to change and savor the excitement with her fellow actors.

It was late, but everyone at Nicole and Marla's was in high spirits. They ate, celebrated, and Brooke was congratulated by one and all.

Rebecca and her husband departed first, but soon after, Troy and his wife, her parents, and Connie and her husband left.

Brooke went to get some more bottled water and a second slice of Marla's German chocolate cake, congratulating herself on managing to be friendly with both Derek and William without speaking alone to either.

She wondered who would leave first.

***

William watched as Brooke moved from one person to another in Nicole's home, graciously accepting congratulations on her performance, joking around with some people, modestly repeating that some of the other actors in the show were more worthy of credit.

"But you did a great job with only a few weeks' time to prepare for the role," Derek said loudly.

William gritted his teeth. Honestly, that guy was so obviously kissing up to Brooke. He sure hoped she could see through Derek's flattery.

She'd been superb, and it was true she'd done it all in a matter of weeks. But did Derek have to keep repeating the same thing? He was a professor. He should come up with something more original.

He watched from the dining room as Nicole handed the guy a scotch and soda. Most of the crowd was drinking soda, water, or coffee. A few people had accepted offers of wine or beer. Derek was the only one who'd asked for a mixed drink of hard liquor. He even looked like a professor, with his tweed-type sports jacket and oxford shirt.

Snob, William thought, then started as Jeremy spoke from behind him.

"Wasn't she great?" Jeremy was obviously proud of his sister. William turned to face him. Jeremy stood behind him, almost in the kitchen doorway.

"Yes, she was," William enthused. "The best one in the show."

"And we're not prejudiced or anything," Jeremy added with a laugh.

"Of course not," William agreed.

Jeremy dropped his voice. "How are you two getting along?"

"Good," William said. "Although Brooke's been so wrapped up in the show, I've hardly seen her. I'm hoping after this weekend, her life will get back to normal, and we can spend time together again. A lot of time."

Jeremy waggled his eyebrows. "That would be very cool," he said. "I think you two go well together."

William hesitated. He felt like he could confide in Jeremy, and he stepped closer towards him, into the kitchen, where they were alone at the moment.

"I'd like to see where our relationship could go," he confided to Jeremy. "I really like your sister. I think, given a chance, it might be something more than friendship."

"Yeah?"

"Yeah," William stated.

Jeremy grinned. "That's great. Of all her boyfriends, I always liked you best, you know."

"Thanks," William said, pleased by Jeremy's confidence. "But, I'm not sure Brooke thinks of me as anything more than a friend."

"I think she does." Jeremy nodded, balancing the plate with a slice of cake on it.

"Good to know," William said. "And…"

"And…?"

"I'm feeling a little guilty."

"Why?" Jeremy wore a perplexed expression.

"I never told her I set up our meeting, that I arranged to 'meet' her by accident, with your help," William said.

Jeremy shrugged. "Do you think she'll care?"

Recalling how Brooke had always said honesty was so important to her, he shifted his position. "I do. I hope she won't get too annoyed."

Jeremy shook his head. "I don't think she will."

"Hope you're right." William took a gulp of his Seven-Up. "I'd hate for her to be mad about it."

"Nah. Brooke has sense. She won't get thrown for a loop by something as minor as you and me setting up your reunion."

William felt some relief. Jeremy knew her well. He smiled. "Thanks."

"Jeremy, we're leaving," said a voice behind William. He turned to regard Rebecca, Jeremy's oldest sister.

Rebecca hugged Jeremy and then turned and gave William a brief hug. "Nice to see you again," she said with a wide smile.

Jeremy and William shook hands with her husband. As they went back to the dining room, William turned slightly.

And found Derek a few yards away, studying him.

He gave Derek a stiff smile.

Derek raised his glass and gave a nod of his head.

Well, that was awkward, William thought.

He hoped Derek hadn't actually heard what he and Jeremy had discussed.

CHAPTER X

By one a.m., the excitement of her performance wore off, and Brooke departed, leaving a handful of other people, including William and Derek, at Nicole's place. She had a suspicion that each of them was waiting for the other to leave first.

She was tired, and the fifteen-minute drive to her home left her comfortably worn and almost ready for bed.

Tiger appeared the minute she walked in the door, and after locking up, she leaned down to pet him. He meowed, as if congratulating her.

"It was a good performance," she told him and went to get him a treat.

She wondered if William and Derek had stayed much longer. Most of the guests left when she did, and she supposed she'd find out from Jeremy how long they'd stayed.

Too tired to check her computer for Facebook or other congratulatory messages, she got ready for bed and quickly fell asleep, satisfied with the evening.

It was late when she woke. She had a leisurely breakfast before checking her email and Facebook page. As she had guessed, she had a slew of messages, most saying she'd been wonderful or from friends who couldn't be there, asking how the performance had gone.

She was almost finished responding when she noticed her answering machine blinking.

The message was from a Mrs. Matisse, who sounded like an older woman. Her cat had died last week, she said, at the age of seventeen. She was hoping to get another cat and wanted to visit with Tiger.

At first, Brooke felt a surge of hope, followed by hesitation.

Would the woman be right for Tiger?

Her thought surprised her. She had wanted a home for him, but now she wanted the *right* home.

She picked up the phone and hesitantly, dialed Mrs. Matisse's number.

They had a nice conversation. Mrs. Matisse lived only half a mile from Brooke, and was a widow whose children were grown. She had had cats all her life and was very familiar with their care. Brooke explained how she'd come to have Tiger. They agreed she would come over in an hour, and Brooke hurriedly got dressed.

Oddly, Tiger had disappeared after breakfast, almost as if he didn't want to meet the woman.

Ridiculous. How could he know about her conversation with Mrs. Matisse?

An hour and ten minutes later Brooke's doorbell rang. Opening the door, she found a gray-haired woman, who looked to be around seventy.

It was obvious from the moment Brooke let her in Mrs. Matisse had been crying.

"I'm sorry I'm—I'm late," she said, sniffling. "I kept thinking of my Boots, and how he would want me to adopt another cat." She paused, and groped in her jacket pocket, removing a handkerchief. "But I…" She blew her nose.

"Please, come in," Brooke said. "Can I get you some water or tea or something?"

"No, thank you, dear." She sniffled again. "I realized on the way here, I'm not ready yet. I want another cat, maybe two, but I don't think I'm ready yet."

"I understand," Brooke said, and patted the woman on the shoulder. "Your cat died…what, a week ago?"

"Nine days," she said, blinking. "I miss him terribly. But I really--think it's too soon for me to get another cat. Maybe in a few weeks…" Her voice trailed off, and she blew her nose again.

Brooke felt an odd mixture of disappointment and relief. This kindly woman seemed to be the type of person she'd want to have Tiger, a concerned and caring pet-owner. On the other hand, Brooke liked having Tiger around and wouldn't mind extending his visit for a few weeks.

"Why don't you call me in a couple of weeks?" Brooke asked. "If he's still here, you can take him home then."

"That's a good idea," Mrs. Matisse said. "Bless you for being so good to this cat."

"Do you want to meet him now?" Brooke asked.

"I'll wait," Mrs. Matisse answered.

After she left, Brooke went back to her computer, sighing. She hoped she'd find a good home for Tiger!

Oddly enough, Tiger showed up about ten minutes after Mrs. Matisse had left.

"You're a strange one," Brooke told him. "You come to the door to see William, but you hide from a potential mom." She sighed again as he leaped into the chair by the window and washed his left front paw.

She finished thanking the people who'd sent her congratulatory notes via email and Facebook, then got ready to go back to the auditorium. They had to put away the sets, gather the costumes to be returned, and do a general clean-up. Afterwards, there was a party at Janice's house, featuring a buffet supper.

The air was filled with a mixture of relief and sadness when they broke down the sets and stored furniture, returned props to their owners, and piled the costumes Janice and Dorothy had volunteered to return. After they finished, Brooke glanced at her cellphone and discovered both Derek and William had called her, as well as Connie and her parents.

She returned Connie's call, then her parents', before driving to the party. She kept the conversations brief, accepting their accolades for her performance.

She decided to call Derek and William back in the evening.

The party was fun, but the weeks of practicing, followed by the weekend's performance, had tired Brooke out. By eight o'clock, she and several other performers thanked and congratulated everyone and left.

Once home, she donned her comfortable old blue flannel pajamas, curled up on the couch, and grabbed her cellphone.

She hesitated for a moment. Who to call first?

She sat still for a moment. She wanted to speak more with William than Derek, she decided. So she'd call Derek and get him out of the way first, then spend more time talking to Will.

Derek answered on the second ring.

He complimented her on the show, then asked if she might be around on Wednesday evening.

"I'm going to be in the area," he said, "giving a lecture to a 'friends of the library' senior citizens group. Can we meet for dinner?"

Usually Brooke exercised on Wednesday, but she could change it for a dinner. "Sure, that would be fine," she told him. She'd like to spend some time with Derek and get to know him better.

They spoke for a few minutes, and then she got off the phone.

Next, she called William.

***

William grabbed the phone when he saw Brooke's name on his display.

"Hey," he greeted her, warmth swirling inside him.

"Hi," she said, and he could hear the smile in her voice.

They spoke about the play first, and he complimented her again on her performance. "You sang so well."

"Thanks, but I played the part before, so it wasn't too difficult."

"Don't be so modest." He relaxed against his desk chair. He'd been at the computer, emailing a friend to catch up. "Everyone did a super job, especially you."

She laughed, her voice light and musical even now. "Thanks."

"How's the cat doing?" he asked when she paused.

She told him about an older woman who had thought about adopting Tiger, since her cat had just died. "But then she decided she wasn't quite ready," Brooke said, sighing. "It's too bad. She would have made a good home for Tiger."

"Maybe she'll be ready soon," he said.

"I hope so." She sounded pessimistic.

They spoke a little more about the cat, and then William invited her out for dinner on Friday. "There's a Thai place not far from my house. Ryan and I tried it last week, and the food was pretty good."

"That sounds great!"

William grinned at her open enthusiasm.

They agreed on a time, and Brooke told him she wanted to go to sleep early. They said goodnight.

William hung up, stretched, then got out of his chair and went into the kitchen.

"Yes!" He punched his fist in the air before opening the refrigerator and taking out a soda.

"Something's got you happy," Ryan said, coming up behind him.

"Brooke. We're going out on Friday," William told his roommate.

"Cool. But, you seem extra happy, buddy."

"I can't help it. I'm looking forward to seeing Brooke already, and I saw her last night," William admitted.

Ryan laughed. "Sounds like love."

Love?

William stared at his friend.

"Love?" he repeated.

"Sure. I haven't seen you this excited about a girl since—since *ever*. Are you in love?" Ryan asked, throwing a water bottle in their recycling bin.

"I-I don't know," he said.

But even as he said the words, he *knew*. "Yes," he admitted suddenly. "I think-yes, I am in love. With Brooke."

"Congrats," Ryan said and hit him on the shoulder. "Hope it goes smoothly."

William grinned back.

Of course it would!

***

After her Jazzercise class, a shower and a late supper, Brooke sat to finish grading papers. She was almost done when her phone rang.

It was William.

"I just wanted to say hi," he said. "I hope I'm not calling too late." It was 9:45.

"No, that's okay," Brooke said. She pushed aside the papers and took her cellphone to the chair by the window, absently smoothing away some cat hair. At the moment, Tiger was sleeping on the carpeted tower she'd set up by the window.

"I was working late, editing an interview with a local mystery writer, and just got home."

"It's nice to hear your voice," she told him. And it was. She leaned back. "Was it an interesting interview?"

"Very. He talked about researching ways to commit murder, hide dead bodies, stuff like that."

She laughed. "Sounds good. I should have done that with Nate," she added without thinking.

"Nate?"

Brooke paused. Why had she mentioned Nate? She had thought about him recently, but that didn't mean she should talk about him to William. On the other hand, she *was* getting closer to William. Maybe she should tell him about her bad experience with Nate.

"Who's Nate?" William asked again.

"Nate was a boyfriend," Brooke said. "He turned out to be married..." She went on, telling him how Nate had deceived her, acted as if he thought she knew he was married, and how she'd finally learned about his concealment of the truth and broken up with the jerk.

William made sympathetic noises as she talked.

"I was really hurt afterwards," she admitted, "and angry. I didn't trust men for a while."

"I can understand that."

"I'm glad you're so honest," she remarked impulsively. She'd never had to worry about that with William.

"Huh? Oh, yeah, that's me," William said with a short laugh.

Was she imagining it or did his voice sound funny? As in funny, peculiar.

Brooke glanced at the carpeted tower where Tiger slept, curled into a ball on the top shelf. Tiger had the right idea. Maybe she was also tired and imagining things.

"That guy was a liar and a cheat," William said with obvious disgust. She must have imagined the odd note in his voice. "You are so much better off without him."

"I know." Brooke smiled. "But at the time, it was traumatic."

"I can see where it would be. Well, I have about another half hour of work to do, so I better get going," William said.

"I'm tired from the weekend and want to turn in early," Brooke admitted. "I'll see you on Friday."

"Goodnight, Brooke."

After they hung up, she stared at her cellphone for a minute.

It had been good to hear William's voice. She liked talking to him. He was a nice guy. Honest, dependable.

She wondered briefly if Derek was like that, too.

Well, as she got to know Derek better, she'd find out.

At least she could count on William.

***

William disconnected the call and stared at his phone.

"I'm glad you're so honest," Brooke had said.

Guilt flooded him.

Honest. Yes, Brooke had always been honest with him—honest with everyone—and had expected honesty from those she cared about.

But he hadn't been totally honest. He remembered discussing it with Jeremy at the party after the show the other evening. He'd felt guilty then. Now he felt doubly so.

Of course, it wasn't that big a deal, he told himself. It wasn't like he'd lied to her about a wife or girlfriend like that jerk, Nate, had, or lied about something important.

He'd just neglected to tell her the whole truth.

Well, he better tell her. Soon. So she knew he was an honest person, one she could really trust.

He'd tell her on Friday, he decided, and got back to work.

***

Derek spoke to the senior citizen's group at the library in Mt. Olive, so it wasn't too far a drive. Brooke met him there and then he followed her to an Italian restaurant she liked a few minutes away. Once they ordered their meals and were served their salads, he told her a little about his projected visit to Egypt.

"Are you worried about the unrest in that part of the world?" Brooke asked, lifting a forkful of lettuce and grape tomatoes.

"No." He shook his head. "I've been there before, and these excavations are well guarded."

She asked him a few questions and sipped some wine. She still had the impression Derek was too wrapped up in himself, although not to the point of being totally self-centered and obnoxious.

Enough to get annoying, she thought ruefully.

Their meals arrived, and Derek dug into his veal marsala while she began eating her chicken parmigiana.

"So, did William tell you the truth?" he asked her suddenly.

"The truth?" Brooke stared at him, puzzled.

"Yeah. I heard him talking to your brother at the party after the show," Derek said.

"What are you talking about?" Brooke felt an uneasy twinge. The truth about what?

Derek reached for his wine. After taking a sip, he placed the glass down with emphasis. Look who's being dramatic, Brooke thought, then swallowed her annoyance.

"I'm talking about what your friend, William, said to your brother. He didn't tell you yet?" Derek made it sound truly awful.

Brooke set her fork and knife down. "Tell me what?" She didn't hide the impatient tone in her voice.

"That William and your brother cooked up some scheme so William could meet you. 'Arranged the meeting by accident' was the way he phrased it."

Ice wedged in her stomach.

CHAPTER XI

"William—and Jeremy—*arranged* my meeting with him?" she choked out.

"Yes." Calmly, Derek speared a piece of mushroom. "Apparently they 'set up' a meeting so William could run into you."

Anger simmered inside Brooke. William—William, who had always been honest—William, who, the other night, she'd complimented on being honest—*had arranged to meet her*?

She thought back to her first meeting with him, only about six weeks ago, at Nicole and Marla's home. How they had joked about the coincidence he was working for the station Nicole's TV show was on. It was so funny they were both at Nicole's for dinner…

It hadn't been a coincidence? "Are you sure?" she demanded, her voice unusually sharp.

Derek nodded. "Yes. Didn't William, or your brother, tell you?" Although he asked the question innocently, the expression in his eyes was far from guileless. It was mischievous. Maybe even cunning.

Suddenly, Brooke was furious. And not just at William. Or Jeremy.

She was mad at Derek, too.

"No, they didn't." She shrugged. She was a better actor than Derek any day. "Not that it's a big deal..." She let her voice dwindle. *But it was a big deal.* At least to her. Honesty—William's honesty, especially after Nate's deception, was so important to her!

"You don't think it's a big deal?" Derek looked disappointed.

"No, I don't." Her voice had taken on a cold note—deliberately. She was mad Derek was attempting to use his knowledge to turn her against William. How juvenile, she thought, and reached for her water glass, taking a few sips, forcing herself not to show her roiling emotions. "If he wanted to meet me so badly he arranged a meeting, what's the harm?" She wished she believed it.

"Oh." Derek looked down, cut up another piece of his meat, then glanced back up. "I thought you'd want to know."

"I appreciate it." She gave him a brief smile. "But it's not a big deal. It's not as if William and I have anything meaningful going." But we could have, she thought. The longing that pierced her was surprisingly intense. *We could have had something special, except now I find out he lied to me.*

She wasn't sure how she managed to get through the remainder of the meal. Her appetite had disappeared and the delicious food no longer tempted her. She managed to make conversation about the places they'd both traveled, but inside, she seethed with anger against William—and also Derek, who acted like a spoiled adolescent, trying to turn her against William for his own benefit.

When Derek suggested dessert, she begged off,

saying she was still tired from the show. She was glad she'd brought her own car. She stayed on while he had coffee, then thanked him and left as soon as he finished his cup.

It started to rain on the ride home. She drove carefully, but was relieved when she reached her condo complex and pulled into her garage. She ran up the stairs, dropped her purse on the coffee table, and threw herself on the couch.

From the hall, Tiger pranced over, jumped on the couch, and settled beside her with a loud purr.

The tension in her eased slightly. She reached out and stroked the cat, wondering what she was going to do.

She was angry and hurt by William's actions. Maybe it was nice he wanted to see her, but why hadn't he told her? Why keep it a secret and deceive her? And Derek! He'd brought this up deliberately, hoping to turn her against William. She gritted her teeth. How childish of him.

She had no desire to see Derek again. She didn't like the games he played, and his self-centeredness turned her off anyway.

All these buzzing thoughts fatigued her.

She got up, dragged herself to her bedroom, and found her oldest, most comfortable flannel pjs. Once she'd dressed for bed, she went back downstairs to watch a little TV.

There was nothing on she wanted to watch. Tiger had disappeared, and she stood by the sliding glass door in her dining room.

Her cellphone rang, but she didn't feel like speaking to anyone, and let it go to voicemail.

Rain now beat steadily against the glass, and a

gust of wind rattled the door. She was certainly glad Tiger wasn't out in this cold, wet weather, fending for himself! On impulse, she went into the kitchen, got him a treat, and left it near his bowl, which was still half-filled with his supper. He preferred to eat several short meals a day, rather than all at once.

He didn't appear, and she decided to go to bed and read there.

Picking up her phone to recharge it, she remembered the earlier call and accessed her voicemail.

"Hi, Brooke." Derek. "I was concerned because you seemed a little…off…this evening. I hope it's just that you're tired and not sick or anything. I'll call you soon."

That was it.

She clicked off her phone. It was nice that Derek had called, but she had a suspicion he knew she was "off" because she was annoyed, not tired; and he was curious to see if he was right.

She had no desire to go out with him anymore.

She went into her study and plugged in her phone to recharge. Tiger slept on her favorite chair. After petting him, she turned off the light and went upstairs.

She opened up her night table drawer, found a book she'd bought a couple of weeks ago she hadn't read yet, and immersed herself in Regency England for a half hour, escaping her own woes. Then she turned off the light and tried to sleep.

But thoughts of William, and how he'd "arranged" the meeting with her, and not told her about it, continued to bombard her mind. Even if he hadn't lied, he'd withheld the truth. How could she trust him?

It was a while before she fell asleep.

***

Brooke didn't sleep well and dragged herself out of bed the next day. She went to work early.

Every time William and his untrustworthy behavior popped into her mind, she firmly pushed the thoughts back. *Not now*. She had work to deal with, and it was a good way to avoid the topic.

She didn't exercise every Thursday, but felt the need to today. Maybe it would help alleviate her frustrations with men. She went to an early evening Jazzercise class. After returning home, she showered, ate, and returned to grading papers. She managed to push both William and Derek from her mind…most of the time.

She entered her grades, then checked her messages. There were two from William, asking her about getting together on Friday.

Did she want to see him? She probably should, if for no other reason than to get things off her chest. And she had a lot to say to him!

There was a hang-up. A quick look at her phone showed it was a call from Derek.

She decided to email William, telling him she'd been very busy all day, but yes, she'd see him tomorrow.

Maybe she should go to his house. Then she could leave whenever she damn well pleased. She suggested she come over after seven, and asked if that would be okay. She knew the area he lived in and could get specific directions from her phone's GPS.

She kept the note short, telling him she'd had a long day of work.

It was nearly ten o'clock. She turned on the TV, and Tiger sprang up on the couch and curled close by her.

She smiled at the cat. At least Tiger could be trusted.

But with a pang, she remembered she was still looking for a home for him. He couldn't really trust *her*.

"I'll find you a *good* home," she vowed.

He stared at her and blinked.

CHAPTER XII

At exactly 7:32, the doorbell rang.

William had paced between his bedroom, his study, and the living room, trying to decide exactly what to say. Ryan had made himself scarce by going to the movies with his girlfriend.

William strode toward the front door and opened it.

Brooke stepped inside the dim vestibule.

"Let me take your jacket," he offered.

She shrugged out of her beige jacket, and he hung it on a peg before closing the door. When she stepped into the living room, he got his first good look at her.

In the bright light, her beautiful green eyes flashed, with what he wasn't sure. He hoped it was gladness to see him, but her jaw looked set, and her mouth wasn't positioned in its usual upturned smile.

"Hi," he said and gave her a quick kiss. Her lips felt stiff beneath his, and she didn't kiss back. He stood straight, studying her beautiful face.

"Hi." Her tone was non-committal.

"Want a soda or something?" he asked. She looked serious. He swallowed. Was something wrong?

"No." She sat on the leather sofa, and he

followed, taking a seat close by. "William, I—I found out something disturbing." She looked him straight in the eyes.

"What? Is someone sick?"

"No." She shook her head. "Someone said…well, did you and Jeremy arrange our 'accidental' meeting at Nicole and Marla's house?" She stared at him, a challenging expression on her face.

Relief poured through him. She'd brought it up. Now it was out in the open.

"As a matter of fact, we did. And I was just about to tell you that tonight—"

She didn't let him finish. "How come you didn't tell me?" Her eyes flashed with anger.

"I was thinking I should," he said calmly, although his heart pounded in his ears. "I'd thought about it quite a bit in the last few weeks, and I decided I should tell you. I started to the other day, when Nicole wanted to talk to you. So—I decided to tell you tonight."

"But you didn't tell me before!" she snapped, her face flushing. "Even when I told you last week how important honesty is to me, when I told you about Nate and how I couldn't trust him or other people—"

"Whoa, whoa," he said, holding up a hand. "I never cheated or lied like that jerk did."

"True, but you didn't tell me the truth. And you *knew* the truth was important to me."

A weird feeling welled up in his gut. Almost…fear. He swallowed. "Brooke," he said, his voice remaining calm, "I know honesty's important to you. That's why I decided to tell you—"

"You should have told me before."

She was being unreasonable. It was his turn to stare. "Look, I didn't, but I intended to tonight, okay? It's not that big a deal. It's not as if I cheated or lied about being married like that jerk, Nate—"

"Not that big a deal? It is to me. I thought…" She paused. When she spoke again, her words came out a harsh whisper. "I thought I could trust you."

"You can. I'm not a liar or a cheat. I didn't tell you Jeremy and I arranged the meeting." He took a breath. "Look, Brooke, when I ran into Jeremy, he asked me to keep it a secret from Nicole that he came from a famous family. Did he tell you that?"

Brooke shook her head. "No, I didn't know he asked you. But I did know he was keeping it a secret."

"Yeah, and it came back to bite him later. In a big way. Anyway, I said I'd keep the secret, in return for a favor. See, I had been thinking about you—a lot. I even dreamed about you. So I asked him if he could find a way to set up a meeting or something, so I could run into you. It was innocent and not something to get bent out of shape about."

"You didn't have to arrange it. You could have simply called." Her voice was still cold.

"Well, this just seemed like a better idea. I thought…I thought it sounded like a more natural way to reconnect. I didn't think about it much. After we started going out, I kept meaning to tell you, but it didn't come up." Or when it had, he'd put it off, he realized. He'd felt those nagging doubts about his putting it off.

"Until now."

"Until now," he repeated, meeting her eyes. "I guess I should have told you sooner, and I'm sorry you learned from someone besides me. How did you find out, anyway?"

She waved her hand. "That's not important."

He stared at her. A memory of the party at Nicole's bounced back in his mind. Derek stood nearby when he and Jeremy talked about how they'd arranged for William and Brooke to meet.

"Derek told you, didn't he?" He ground out the words.

"It doesn't matter. I learned about it, and I was upset you didn't tell me the truth—"

"It's not that big a deal," he repeated.

"It is to me!" Brooke shot up from her seat. "I need to know the man I'm dating is trustworthy. After my experience with Nate, I need to know I can depend on you to tell the truth."

"You can," he said firmly.

"How can I?"

"Because you can." He hated to see tears in her eyes. He stood and reached for her.

She stepped backwards.

"I can't." The tone of her voice was adamant. "If you lied to me once, you could do it again."

"I didn't lie." Why was she making such a big deal about this?

"Almost." She took another step back.

"Brooke." He stopped and ran a hand through his hair. "I care about you. More than that." He stopped again. He might as well say it. "I love you."

"No." She shook her head. "You don't. And even if you did, I can't trust you."

"Yes, I do," he said. "And you *can* trust me." But as he looked at her distraught expression, he wondered if he had made a mistake telling her about his love. Maybe this wasn't the time.

"I better go." She grabbed her purse and coat and hurried to the door.

"Brooke!" He strode after her.

"I need to think." She grabbed the handle, pulled the door open, and ran out without another word.

William stared at her retreating figure as she ran through the darkness to her car.

What the heck was wrong with her? Why was she overreacting? True, he hadn't told her the whole truth, but it wasn't as if he'd lied! He certainly hadn't done what that snake Nate had done.

She started the motor. He sprinted forward to stop her. "Brooke!"

But she'd already turned on the headlights and backed out of the driveway.

***

Brooke sniffled, but managed to stem the tears until she got home. Once inside, they flowed down her cheeks. She threw herself on the couch in the living room and cried in the dark.

Why hadn't William told her he'd arranged their meeting? Why had he—maybe not lied, exactly, but not told the complete truth? Could she ever trust him? She didn't want to get close to a man she didn't trust. And she couldn't trust him. Just like Nate.

But no, part of her mind argued. He didn't outright lie like Nate…

But she still couldn't trust him.

At some point, she became aware Tiger snuggled

beside her. She sat up and placed the cat on her lap. He purred as she stroked him.

"You want me to feel better, don't you?" she asked, reaching for a tissue and wiping her eyes.

He purred again, jumped off her lap, sat, and washed his front right paw as if he thought she'd had enough sympathy.

Brooke got up, emotionally spent. All she wanted was to go to sleep.

She washed her hot face with cold water, then got into her favorite flannel pajamas. She didn't want to read or watch TV. She thought of calling Connie, but decided to simply go to sleep instead. Maybe she'd feel better in the morning.

When she did fall asleep, it wasn't restful. She dreamt Nate and William both chased her in cars, and she sped in her car, trying to get away from them.

She was awake before eight o'clock—early for a Saturday. Brooke fed Tiger, made coffee and picked at some oatmeal, wondering what she would do the rest of the day. Maybe she would go see Jeremy later.

She showered, and dressed in old, comfortable jeans and a worn light blue sweatshirt.

When she came downstairs, Tiger waited at the bottom, looking up at her.

"Oh, you're cute," she said, and bending down, scooped him up. She carried him to the chair in her home office and sat, stroking the cat.

Sunshine poured in through the window on this bright Saturday morning, though the weather forecast predicted a chilly day.

Tiger purred, content in her arms with sunlight hitting his body.

"You like it here, don't you?" Brooke asked him. "And I like having you around."

The realization hit her square in her stomach.

She *liked* having Tiger around. She really did. In the weeks since he'd come to live with her, she'd enjoyed him, enjoyed his quirks and companionship, the occasional demands for attention, and his comforting presence.

In fact, she'd fallen for the cat.

"I love you, you silly cat," she said, realization striking her again.

He looked at her with his light green eyes and gave a loud purr.

"You love me too, don't you?" she asked and laughed as he stared at her. "We make a good team. You know that?" As he continued to stare at her, she made up her mind. "You're staying with me. This is your forever home now, buddy. I hope you're happy."

In answer, he gave a loud, satisfied purr.

She petted the cat, amazed at how he'd grown on her. She enjoyed having him around. She couldn't imagine living without him now. He had a place in her heart. And she didn't want to give him up. Little by little, he'd claimed her heart, and she knew she loved him.

And on the heels of that thought came another one, like the curtain rising on a new play.

Little by little, just as gradually, William had claimed a place in her heart.

She loved him. In the last few months, their friendship had become increasingly important to her and had turned to something more. To love!

She'd thought love meant being swept off her feet, the way it had happened to her parents. Her love for William had come slowly, gradually. Like her soft-footed cat. Maybe it had even been building when they were young.

Now, it was full-blown.

And it hurt. Because she felt an ache in her middle. An ache because she had hurt him, had turned him away when he had confessed his love to her.

She groaned, and Tiger looked at her quizzically.

"What am I going to do?" she asked the cat.

What *was* she going to do? William had declared his love, and she'd walked away from him.

How could she have been so stupid?

One thought rapidly followed another, all of them crystal clear.

She hadn't trusted him. All because of her bad experience with Nate. But William was his own man. He had never given her one reason to feel he wasn't worthy of trust.

She wanted to slap herself in the head and nearly did. What is wrong with you, Brooke Alicia Perez? You shouldn't judge one person because of the actions of another!

Geez, she was acting as erratic as Nicole had when she was upset because Jeremy hadn't told her the truth about his famous family. And that was a bigger concealment of a fact than what William had done in hiding the truth about how they met.

She had gone to Nicole then and asked her to give Jeremy a second chance. And Nicole had.

Without another thought, she set Tiger gently on his favorite chair, so he could bask in the sunlight. Then she grabbed the phone. She needed Nicole's advice now.

Nicole picked up on the second ring.

"Nicole?"

"What's wrong?" Nicole asked when she heard Brooke's tremulous voice.

"I had a fight with William, and it's my fault," Brooke admitted. "Can I come over and talk?"

"Sure. Jeremy's working part of the day, and I'm here baking brownies. Come right over."

Brooke thanked her, hung up, and paused to give Tiger a treat. Then she hurried to grab her purse.

Brooke reached Nicole's house in record time. Sitting at Nicole's kitchen table, she poured out her story as Nicole made a fresh pot of coffee and took the brownies out of the oven.

"So, I realized I loved William," Brooke concluded, sighing. "And I messed it up."

Nicole added milk and sugar and handed Brooke a mug. Stirring the same ingredients into her own coffee, she perched on a chair near Brooke.

"It's not too late to fix things," she said soothingly. "I should know. The same thing happened to me and Jeremy not even a month ago. Remember?"

Brooke inhaled the rich aroma from the coffee, spiked by the delicious scent of the cooling brownies. "I know. Do you really think I haven't wrecked our relationship?"

"If he loves you—and judging by what I've seen, he does—he'll give you another chance," Nicole said. "First of all, William seems like a caring guy who would be forgiving, even if you did hurt his feelings. And second, if he loves you, he'll give you another chance."

Brooke sipped the warm brew. It tasted rich and

soothing as it slid down her throat. "I have to try," she said.

"Yes. He may try to get in touch, but I think you need to go to him and tell him your feelings," Nicole suggested. "He doesn't know you love him yet."

"I need a grand gesture, kind of what you and Jeremy did," Brooke mused, recalling how they'd each called her about making meals for the other.

"Cooking a meal for him?" Nicole asked, furrowing her brow.

"No, something more personal, from me. Something like…oh, setting the stage." An idea sparked in her mind. "I could set the stage for romance!"

"How?" Nicole asked eagerly.

"I could use the stage at Quemby. There's nothing going on there tonight, just a string ensemble this afternoon." She thought for a moment. "Maybe I could get that tower we used for last year's production of Romeo and Juliet…" Her voice trailed off. She shook her head. "No, that would be hard to set up by myself, and I don't want to involve anyone else."

"There must be some other romantic setting you could use on stage," Nicole urged.

"I could read a romantic poem. You know, like 'How do I Love Thee' by Elizabeth Barrett Browning," Brooke said.

"That's romantic," Nicole agreed. "We could easily get a copy of it from the internet, but I may actually have it in a book of poetry."

"Or maybe I could print it out, leave it on a desk center stage, and then read it to him," Brooke said, warming to the idea. "Complete with a red rose…and maybe some brownies."

"Men love food." Nicole grinned.

Brooke rushed on. "There's a small desk and chair I could easily drag on stage. And if you would help me make some brownies…?"

"Of course. You could use the ones I've made—"

"No, I want to make my own," Brooke said, shaking her head.

They stirred up another batch of brownies, found the poem online and printed it.

By this time, Marla, who had worked the night before, was awake, and she pitched in, helping to ice the brownies and then wrap them up with a red bow around the container Brooke borrowed. Brooke hugged both sisters and thanked them effusively, then drove to a nearby florist where she purchased a red rose.

As she left the store, she realized she hadn't even called William yet. For all she knew, he was working.

She sat in her car for a moment. How should she handle contacting him? She decided the surprise would be best if she texted him. Of course, speaking on the phone would be more inviting, because she could put emphasis and sincerity into her words. But she was looking for a certain element of surprise.

So she texted him.

"I gave a lot of thought to what happened last night. I'd like to discuss the situation with you. Please meet me at the Quemby Theatre at six o'clock. I'll leave the back stage door unlocked. I hope you can be there."

She paused, then sent the text before she changed her mind.

She hoped he responded. Soon.

CHAPTER XIII

Brooke drove home and arrived a little before two o'clock. It was too early to go to Quemby, so she had a small, late lunch, then watched TV with Tiger on the couch. She couldn't help constantly checking her cell phone.

At a quarter to three, her phone chimed a text had been received, and she grabbed it.

"I'll be glad to meet you," it read. "Why Quemby? Are you working in the theater this afternoon?"

She sagged with relief. William was willing to meet her! A smile burst on her face, and she felt as light as air.

She hesitated for a second. She didn't want to spoil the surprise, so she merely answered, "I'll see you there at six." and sent the message.

Now, if only he reacted the way she hoped he would.

She had time to relax, but she found herself flipping through TV stations, unable to concentrate on any one program. Finally, she curled up with her book and spent a little time reading about Regency balls and British spies.

By four o'clock, she sprang into action. She changed to her gray knit dress, the blue, green and gray scarf and blue earrings Derek had liked that she wished she'd worn for William. Spritzing herself with perfume, she decided she looked feminine in the outfit. It was getting chilly as the sun drew closer to the horizon. She fed Tiger, then scrounged in the closet for her nice black boots. She pulled on a navy blue coat.

She left the condo shortly after five. She could hear the firmness in her step as her boots clicked against the sidewalk, and she couldn't help the hopeful smile forming on her face. The air was cold, but still, and felt soothing against her warm cheeks.

She was hopeful as she listened to the radio and drove to the college. Once there, she scooped up the things she'd brought with her. She had her key in her hand, but discovered the backdoor to the auditorium was still unlocked. She brought in the rose, brownies, and printed copies of the poem.

Inside, she found a couple of people, including Geraldo, finishing the clean-up after the string concert.

"Hi, Brooke," he said.

"Hi! Geraldo, can you and Dan move that small desk on the left side of the storeroom out to the middle of the stage, if you don't mind? I'll get the chair." Having them here would make it easy to set the stage for love.

"Sure thing." He regarded her. "What's up?"

She smiled. "Just a little skit I'm practicing with someone."

"Sure." He hefted a couple of music stands. "These are the last of them, Dan." He carried them into the area they used for musical supplies.

Brooke went into the actor's quarters and found the simple desk chair.

All the time, her heart hammered.

She had the chair set up by the desk when Geraldo announced they were finished.

"We'll lock the front doors and leave the back door open," he said. "The janitor is still working in the lobby."

"Okay, have a nice evening," Brooke told him.

"You, too."

She glanced at her watch. Just after five-thirty. She grabbed her "props" and carefully laid out the rose, the brownies, and the poem in an inviting way on the small desk. She checked herself in one of the actors' room's mirrors, then went to the tech area where she turned on the microphone, set the stage lights to dim, and sat. To wait for William.

The janitor appeared to have finished sweeping, and she didn't see him out in the audience area anymore. So the front door was probably locked. She grabbed her cellphone and hurriedly checked to see the back door was still open and no one had locked it. When she'd satisfied herself that all was in order, she returned to the tech booth.

She guessed he was driving to the college by now. She glanced at her watch again. 5:42.

She really had to stop being so nervous. She kept herself from staring at her watch, but two looks showed her it was 5:48 and then 5:52.

A sudden noise in the back, followed by footsteps, alerted her.

"Brooke?" William called.

He was early! Was he as eager as she was? She

heard his footsteps drawing closer as he approached the stage.

"Please take a seat at the desk on stage." She made her voice cheerful as she spoke into the mic.

Slowly, William walked onto the stage. He glanced around, puzzlement on his face. "Brooke?" he repeated. He looked up, staring towards the back of the theatre and the audio visual booth.

And, as she watched, he paused, focusing on the rose, the folded paper, and the open plastic bin with the brownies on the desk.

He approached the desk, reached into the plastic bin and took a brownie, and bit into it.

Brooke swallowed. Typical man, she thought with some exasperation. Food first!

She spoke into the mic again. "Sit down, and when you're finished eating the brownie, please listen." She strove to make her voice pleasant and not nervous.

He finished chewing, touched the red rose, and focused on the sound and lighting room. As she watched him, he stared up and waved.

She stilled her hand to keep from waving back. This was serious.

"Hi," he called out.

"Hi," she said into the mic, unable to help responding. Her voice sounded breathless to her own ears. "Have a seat."

William sat behind the desk. He touched the rose again, then looked up at her.

"I'd like to read you something," she said. "If you'd like to follow along, there's a print out on the pages in front of you."

William reached for the crisp white papers and unfolded them.

Brooke swallowed as butterflies flew about her stomach. Then, making a strong effort to keep her voice calm and appealing, she began.

"This is from one of the most powerful love poems of all time, written by Elizabeth Barrett Browning," she began. She paused, then launched into the verse, which she had practically memorized in the last few hours. Still, she had her copy spread in front of her.

"How do I love thee? Let me count the ways…"

He stared down at the papers in front of him, and a smile overtook his face. Happy flutters cascaded around her stomach now. He looked…happy! And glad!

"I love thee freely," Brooke continued, her voice remaining melodious. When she reached the final line of the poem, tears pricked her eyes.

"I shall but love thee…." She finished the poem, and her voice drifted off, the sweet tones hanging in the air with the drama of the words that concluded the verse.

A tear broke free and wound down her cheek. She wiped it away and finished. "That poem was written over a hundred years ago by Elizabeth Barrett Browning to her future husband, Robert. It describes my feelings for you, William, better than I can. I love you."

William stood and strode forward. He vaulted off the stage and hurried up through the theatre towards the sound and lighting room.

Brooke didn't wait. She ran out of the room and met him halfway.

"Brooke!" he exclaimed as she neared him. "I love you!" He grabbed her in his arms and swung her around. Setting her down, he kissed her soundly.

When she came up for air, Brooke smiled at him through her tears. William pulled back and beamed down at her.

"I was so afraid last night that I blew our whole relationship, since I didn't admit about setting us up," he blurted. "I barely slept. I kept trying to think about ways to win you over. I was planning to go to your house tonight and plead for another chance."

"It's my fault," Brooke told him. "I made a whole big mountain out of a small molehill. I can see you wanted an opportunity to see me again, and, well—I blew the incident out of proportion. I guess it's because of my experience with Nate but—oh, it doesn't matter. I realized I love you, William. I love you and I always will!"

Once again, his lips met hers, and she felt the sizzle all the way to the tips of her toes.

William pulled back and sighed happily. "This is the best moment of my life." He grinned at her.

She smiled back. "Me, too. I was hoping if I set the stage for love, you would forgive me."

"There's nothing to forgive," he said firmly. "Just one more question to ask."

She raised her eyebrows.

"Will you marry me, Brooke? I want to spend my life with you."

Direct and succinct, that was her William. Through misty eyes, Brooke smiled up at him. "Yes, as long as you're okay with having a cat tag along. I realized I loved Tiger, too. You both grew on me before I knew it!"

He smiled and pulled her close again. "I've grown fond of him, too. It's a deal." He nuzzled her. "I love him almost as much as I love you."

They kissed again, forgetting the stage, the setting, and everything but the fact that they loved each other.

EPILOGUE

"They look so happy!" Brooke exclaimed.

Standing next to Marla, she wiped a tear from her eye as they watched Nicole and Jeremy gliding around the dance floor for their first dance as Mr. and Mrs. Jeremy Perez.

The wedding ceremony had been beautiful, and Brooke had shed a few happy tears, along with Marla. Now, as she and Marla and several of Nicole's friends stood to the side in their rose-colored dresses, waiting for the deejay to call the entire wedding party to the dance floor, she smiled at her brother and his new bride. Nicole and Jeremy were deeply in love, and the beautiful July afternoon had lent itself to a wonderful church wedding with pictures outside in the park before they'd arrived at the reception.

Nicole and Jeremy weren't the only happy ones, Brooke thought, as she met William's eyes across the floor.

He stood with the other groomsmen, waiting until the entire wedding party would be announced again and they could dance together. Brooke wiggled her fingers, and the beautiful round diamond ring on her finger flashed in the lights from the chandeliers above.

Their own wedding was scheduled for November, right after Thanksgiving. They were going to go away for a few days, then take a prolonged cruise to several Caribbean islands in January, when Brooke was between semesters. Jeremy and Nicole had decided to go to Italy, with a brief stay on the island of Capri and some sightseeing in Florence, Rome, and Venice.

And they weren't the only ones getting married! Marla and Scott had become engaged last month and were planning a wedding for next spring. They were all going to be attendants in each others' weddings, since the three couples had remained close friends.

William winked. She smiled back, joyful that she would soon be marrying the man she loved.

She caught Jeremy's eye as he moved around the dance floor with Nicole. She'd never seen him look so happy. He had a surprise for Nicole, too, and Brooke and their siblings were in on it. The four would be singing a song just for Nicole later during the reception—with Jeremy in the lead and his sisters and brother singing back-up. He wanted to sing the Todd Rundgren song, "I Saw the Light in Your Eyes" to Nicole. He'd rehearsed several times with Brooke and their siblings, and she knew Nicole would be surprised and thrilled.

When the first dance, "Always and Forever," ended, the guests burst into applause. Brooke caught sight of her parents and Nicole's, smiling proudly as they stood near the dance floor.

"And now we invite the parents of our bride and groom, Sharon and Rafael Perez and Donna and Paul Vitarelli, to join the happy couple on the dance floor... and our attendants, maid of honor Marla Vitarelli; best man Troy Perez; bridesmaids Brooke Perez, Kathy…" he continued.

As the ushers were announced, William waited until his name was read, and then he came forward to claim Brooke for the dance.

"What should our first song be?" he murmured in her ear.

"I have a couple of ideas," she answered, snuggling close.

"I can't wait," he said.

She smiled. "I'm so glad you decided to try to get together with me again, William."

He pulled back to gaze down lovingly at her face. "And I'm glad you set the stage for our love, Brooke." He tightened his hold.

And as they danced, Brooke knew they would always dance through the stages of life together, no matter what the scene!

THE END

ABOUT THE AUTHOR

Roni Denholtz has published 8 novels and one novella. Her books have been nominated for the New Jersey Golden Leaf Award and the National Readers' Choice Award. "Marquis in a Minute" won the NJ Golden Leaf award for Best Regency Romance. She has also written dozens of short stories and articles for magazines such as "Baby Talk," "Child Life," and "For the Bride." She is the author of 9 children's books, published by January Productions. "Jenny Gets Glasses" was named #7 of the Top Twenty Favorite Books of First Graders in a nationwide study by the Reading is Fundamental Group.

A former special education teacher, Roni also taught "Writing for Fun and Profit" in her local adult school for many years and some of her students went on to get published.

Roni is a member of New Jersey Romance Writers, where she served as president for the 2016 year; Romance Writers of America; and the Authors Guild. When her children were younger, she also was active in Marching Band Parents, Robotics Parents, and PTA.

Roni and her husband own an independent real estate company, Jersey Success Realty, in northwestern New Jersey. They have two grown children and a rescue dog. Roni served on the board of Noah's Ark Animal Shelter for 8 years..

She is an avid reader, and enjoys photography, cooking and travel.

She loves to hear from readers! Find her on facebook and on her webpage at www.ronidenholtz.com

Made in the USA
Middletown, DE
25 February 2021

34411749R00099